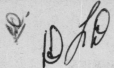

PLAYIN' POSSUM

Cursing, Slocum found a small space between two prickly pear pads big enough to shoot—and see—through. There was no sign of that bastard Crowfoot. Cold, hard rage coursed through Slocum. He just aimed at a clump of vegetation large enough to hide a man—and fired three times.

Returned shots spattered into the cactus mere inches from his head, and sent prickly thorns into his cheek. Ignoring the pain, Slocum fired twice at the next largest clump, the one from which the shots had come. This time, cactus exploded and he heard a faint yelp. No shots were returned. But Crowfoot was a tricky sonofabitch—he could very well be playing possum, waiting for Slocum to come check on him. But Slocum was taking no chances.

Jeb Crowfoot, bleeding from his thigh, was busy tying off the wound with a fresh handkerchief. He swore. This was supposed to be an easy job. It was why he'd broken his rule about never going to the same place twice . . .

JAKE LOGAN

HOLDING DOWN
THE RANCH

JOVE BOOKS, NEW YORK

HOLDING DOWN THE RANCH

A Jove Book / published by arrangement with
the author

PRINTING HISTORY
Jove edition / November 2003

Copyright © 2003 by Penguin Group (USA) Inc.

For information address: The Berkley Publishing Group,
a division of Penguin Group (USA) Inc.,
375 Hudson Street, New York, New York 10014.

ISBN: 0-515-13632-8

A JOVE BOOK®
Jove Books are published by The Berkley Publishing Group,
a division of Penguin Group (USA) Inc.,
375 Hudson Street, New York, New York 10014.
JOVE and the "J" design
are trademarks belonging to Penguin Group (USA) Inc.

PRINTED IN THE UNITED STATES OF AMERICA

10 9 8 7 6 5 4 3 2 1

1

"Hey, you! Ain't you Slocum?" called the voice, much too young and much too full of itself to do anybody any good.

Reluctantly, Slocum looked toward the sound. It was just as he had suspected. The boy was seventeen—and that was stretching it some—barely shaving, shortish, yellow-haired, and standing across the street in an all-too-familiar stance.

Everybody else on the street had recognized the boy's stance, too—legs wide, arms curled toward his six-guns, and his face cocky and intense, albeit nervous—because they commenced to scatter like flies off a screen door.

Slocum hefted his parcel to his left arm and called back, "You're mistaken, son," while two men and a mangy dog ducked back into the mouth of an alley.

The last thing Slocum needed was some wet-behind-the-ears Quick Draw Johnny lying dead in the street. If this kid was intent on getting himself killed, let somebody else do it. Slocum had better things to do. For instance, take this yardage of red silk up to the delightful Miss Tansy Sykes. She'd been waiting for it for weeks.

"Don't think I am," the boy called. His voice hitched a little. "You're him, all right."

The fingers on the boy's right hand twitched nervously, underscoring his uncertainty. "I'm callin' you out, Slocum."

"Don't push it, kid," Slocum warned just as the last matron on the street, dragging a reluctant ten-year-old, dived into a shop front a half block up the way. "You're gettin' yourself into more trouble than you want to know."

"Draw," shouted the boy, a whole lot louder than necessary.

"Your nerves are showin'," replied Slocum. "Why don't you go on home?"

In reply, the boy drew.

But Slocum drew faster.

He winged the kid in his gun arm before the boy had cleared leather all the way, and the boy's gun went flying off to the side, shattering a storefront window. Simultaneously, the boy folded, dropped to his knees, and gripped his arm. He had a very surprised look on his face and a whimper on his trembling lips.

Slocum holstered his gun. He still had the brown paper package of yard goods tucked securely under his left arm. He looked up and down the vacant street, sighed, shook his head, then called out, "Somebody want to get this kid to the doc? You got a doc in this town, don't you?"

A bald head poked out the door of the general store, followed tentatively by the scrawny body attached to it.

"I-I'll see to it, Mister Slocum," the man said hesitantly. Then added, "Are you *really* Sloucm? *The* John Slocum?"

"Never heard of him, buddy," Slocum replied, and walked on up the street toward Tansy Sykes's place. Behind him, he heard opening doors and folks coming out of their hiding places, and the murmur of excited conversation.

He tried not to listen.

But he knew one thing: No matter how much he denied his name, he was on borrowed time here in Bedrock.

Damn that kid, anyhow!

"Who was he?" Tansy said distractedly as she took the package from him. They were upstairs in her room, which was still disheveled from their marathon lovemaking.

Tansy wasn't much better off, as she was still in her robe. She tore back the package's corner and squealed, "Oh, it's gorgeous! I been waiting for this silk for 'bout a whole month!"

"Don't know who he was," said Slocum, just as she stood on her tiptoes and threw her arms around his neck.

"Thanks for pickin' it up, honey!" she whispered into his ear, just before her teeth nipped its lobe. "Oh, I'm gonna be splendiferous in this, don't you think? I'm gonna send for the dressmaker right away!"

That was one thing about his Tansy, Slocum thought with a grin. She had her priorities.

He'd pulled into Bedrock three days prior and run into Tansy by accident—well, he went in the Bedrock Saloon, and she was there, just like she'd been waiting for him—and other than a few quick trips down to the livery to check on Concho, he hadn't come back outside its doors until about noon today.

He was sort of surprised that Tansy could still walk.

As a matter of fact, he was a little surprised that he could, too.

And now here she was, nibbling at his ear again. "You game, big boy?" she whispered.

"Always am," he said with a growl, and pulled her close.

She gave a little gasp of surprise, but she was grinning. She was dusky and dark, with a husky voice with a figure that would have put Venus herself to shame.

Slocum had met her three years before in a little mining

town up north. As he recalled, that meeting had resulted in a five-day marathon that left him grinning like a fool for a fortnight.

He wondered if he could stretch this visit out long enough to equal it.

She wasn't wearing anything under her robe. Slocum spread the pale blue silk and slid his hands beneath it to touch warm, soft flesh the color of creamed coffee. They traveled over a tiny waist, swept down to belled hips, then back up to cup full, heavy, round breasts. Her fingers, long and elegant, moved slowly down his chest and to his belt buckle.

"Just where you goin', honey?" he asked with an ornery grin.

"As if you didn't know," she purred. She reached inside and took him, growing rapidly, in her hand. "My big, strong, handsome Slocum," she murmured against his lips. "Bigger all the time."

He took her against the wall, and she wrapped her long legs around his hips while he plunged into her—slowly at first, then faster and faster, then slowly again, until she was so crazed with passion that she begged him to please, please finish it before she went mad.

He quickened his pace once more, going ever deeper, and just when the fire in his own loins brightened, then flared into a heady bonfire, she exploded into her own climax.

He slumped against her, holding her up while she trembled mindlessly in the throes of it, even though he was barely able to stay on his feet. Resting his head on the dark softness of her shoulder, he puffed out his cheeks and exhaled through pursed lips.

Sometimes, at times like this, he wondered what it would be like to be a gal. It was brief, but he did wonder. They always came so . . . all out. Just lost their senses.

For him, it was pretty damned fine, too, but he never

went into the sun or anything. That was how Tansy had described it. Like flying and soaring and spinning, and going right into the heart of the sun.

She relaxed, and he let her slide down to stand on the floor.

She stroked his cheek. "Slocum," she purred, slit-eyed as a tabby cat full of fresh cream. "You'll singe my wings."

"Tansy, honey, I—" He stopped midsentence, and they both turned their heads toward the door. Somebody was pounding on it.

"We're busy in here, if you don't mind," Tansy shouted.

Unfortunately, she shouted it directly into Slocum's ear. He stuck a finger into it, but it was too late.

"Oops," Tansy said belatedly. "Sorry."

"Open up, Miss Tansy!" came the voice again, along with a series of serious knuckle raps.

Slocum reached down and pulled up his britches and his gunbelt, buckling both hurriedly. As he handed Tansy her robe, he growled, "Hang on a minute, there, buddy."

But they didn't. They broke the door in.

There in the hall stood a squat little man, pink-skinned as a newborn baby, clean shaven, and sporting a tin badge. Behind him stood a somewhat taller, much thinner galoot in a hat that looked two sizes too big for him. He had tin on his shirt, too.

It seemed that once they had the door caved in, they were stumped for what to do next, because they just stood there. The taller fellow, the one Slocum figured to be the deputy, swallowed several times, his Adam's apple bobbing nervously up and down.

Slocum just stood there, too, looking at them and waiting. The expression on his face wasn't any too kind, either.

Tansy, back in her robe again, stepped between the

men. "Bill Hawkins, have you lost all your manners?" she asked. Then she glanced at the man behind him. "Afternoon, Joey."

The deputy briefly touched the brim of his too-large hat. "Miss Tansy, ma'am," he said softly, and a little shyly.

Sheriff Bill Hawkins was still staring at Slocum. Something flickered over his features—Slocum couldn't tell exactly what—and then Hawkins breathed, "You *are* him, ain't you?"

"Depends on who you're lookin' for," Slocum replied testily. He didn't want a gunfight, and he sure as hell didn't want to have one upstairs at the Bedrock Palace. But if this idiot pushed him hard enough, he'd push back.

Hawkins seemed to come back from wherever his mind had been floating, and cleared his throat. "Tall, dark hair, green eyes, powerful build, got an Appaloosa down to the livery . . . Yeah, you're Slocum, all right," he said, a little too forcefully. "We're lookin' for the man who shot young Al Childers out front of the dry goods about a half-hour ago. It was you, wasn't it, Slocum?"

Curtly, Slocum nodded his head, although he was a little surprised that the sheriff had so much information on him so close at hand, right down to the Appaloosa.

"That'd be me," Slocum said. "And that was a wild kid, lookin' for a reputation, Sheriff. He drew on me. I didn't have anything in my hand but this." He grabbed the parcel he'd brought to Tansy from the tabletop and held it forward.

With his left hand, of course. He kept the right one free, just in case.

"You must'a had something, Mr. Slocum," the deputy piped up. "Poor Al was all shot up."

Tansy drew herself up. "Well, Slocum shot in self-defense, didn't you, honey? And *I* could outdraw Al Childers."

One corner of Slocum's mouth quirked up and he whispered, "Gee, thanks, Tansy."

She snatched the scarlet yardage from him, muttering, "I'm only trying to help, dammit."

"Either way, he's shot," said the sheriff stubbornly. And, Slocum thought, a little apologetically.

"Now, I'm askin' you, Slocum," the sheriff went on, "and I'm askin' you as nice as I know how—to get out of my town."

"On what grounds?" Slocum shot back. "There's no paper out on me."

The sheriff swallowed, hard. "On . . . on the grounds that if Al Childers got himself a slug in the arm, he won't be the only one gettin' shot up. Fellers like you—fellers with a reputation for bein' fast and tough, you know? They draw trouble like sugar-syrup draws in flies."

"For this," interjected Tansy, "you had to break down my door?"

"We was at a fever pitch, ma'am," explained the deputy. "That is," he added, blushing, "till we seen he was actually in here. You sure look pretty today, ma'am."

Tansy, tousled and barely dressed, snorted and rolled her eyes.

Sharply, Sheriff Hawkins elbowed his deputy in the ribs. "Now, Slocum," he said, "I'm askin' you nice. I know damn well that you could kill us both before we cleared leather. I'll make no beans about that. But the citizens of Bedrock voted me in to keep them free of shoot-outs in the street and the like. And, well, I figure you're kind of a magnet for 'em."

Slocum couldn't disagree, and he had to admit that he was a little impressed with what the sheriff had just said. Most places, the constabulary would simply hide in an alley and try to backshoot him when he wasn't looking.

He knew he'd best move along. Staying around was going to be a whole lot more trouble than it was worth.

Even considering Tansy.

So Slocum said, "All right. I'll cut out this afternoon."

Tansy's eyebrows flew up a good half inch. "You'll *what*?"

No one looked more surprised than the sheriff, though, although his deputy came in a close second. "You will?" asked Sheriff Hawkins. It seemed he had halfway expected a heated shoot-out.

"Really?" asked the bewildered deputy.

"Jesus," muttered Slocum, and picking up his saddlebags, grabbed Tansy around the waist. "Goodbye, baby," he said, and kissed her.

"You're sure one surprisin' son of a buzzard," he heard the sheriff say.

Slocum just waved him off.

2

Slocum reined Concho down into the arroyo, then up and out the other side. It was a nice day, despite having been kicked out of Bedrock—the third such town he'd been kicked out of in less than three weeks.

Of course, in some of those places the kicking-out had been a little more literal.

And he was beginning to wonder why, all of a goddamn sudden, every two-bit gunman, quick-draw-Johnny, and kid with a slingshot in the Arizona Territory was so hot to leave him dead in the street.

It wasn't as if he'd been in a fight with anybody famous lately. That was what usually triggered a chain of events like this, like the bad six months he'd spent after he'd taken out Toby Gassman up in Montana, or the tough three months in California after he'd shot Bad Bob Billings.

Hell, they'd been jumping out from underneath every rock and bush there for a while.

He reined Concho around a prickly pear patch, and scared up a covey of quail in the process. The parents darted off, crested heads bobbing, their young trailing behind like a series of those wind-up toys the drummers sold.

Concho, however, wasn't disturbed in the least, and merely nodded his head to match his gait, never breaking the slow, steady rhythm of it. That was one thing Slocum liked about the tall, chestnut, leopard Appaloosa—he didn't have a spooky bone in his body. Of course, the gelding didn't have much "jump" in him, but you couldn't have everything.

Slocum figured that Concho's surefootedness over bad terrain, his steadiness when other horses would fly off the handle and run for cover—and the not-incidental fact that he was one of the best reining and even-gated horses that Slocum had ever had the pleasure to ride—more than made up for his lack of speed.

Then again, maybe if Concho had a good reason to really run flat out, he would. Slocum had never pushed the issue with either his spurs or his quirt. No sense in it.

He came to a fork in the trail, reined up Concho, and sat there for a moment in the late afternoon sun, considering. He was at loose ends, and he could go any way he wanted. Elk City was to the southwest, Indian Springs was to the north, or he could ride due south to Plumville.

But then, Elk City wasn't more than a wide spot in the road, as he recalled. Their silver had given out years ago, and most of the population had given out along with it.

Plumville was a going concern, though, as he remembered. Several saloons, three whorehouses—and a sheriff who wasn't nearly so thoughtful as Hawkins, back in Bedrock.

Slocum wasn't in the mood for trouble, not right at the moment.

After a few moments of further internal debate, he reined Concho north, toward Indian Springs.

Last month he'd finished up a job for Roy Tanner,

down along the border, and had been wandering ever since. Wandering with six hundred dollars in his pocket, he would have hastened to add, had he been asked.

Well, it had started out as six hundred. Now, it was more like two-fifty or so. It would have been more if he hadn't gotten into that poker game back in Sawdust, but there you were.

A man had a right, he guessed, to spend his money any way he wanted, even if he gambled it away like a damned fool.

He contented himself that the next time or the time after, he'd come out richer than he went in. Poker was like that. He'd planned on having a little fun gaming back in Bedrock, too, but then, he hadn't counted on Tansy being there. And Tansy had been more fun than a game of cards, anyhow.

In Indian Springs, he'd stick to pasteboards, though. Pasteboards, a good cigar or three, and some fine champagne. Now, those would fit the bill, wouldn't they?

Tansy's place had been short of good cigars, and they hadn't seen any champagne in there since the rail was laid. Which was why, come to think of it, he'd spent most of his time up in Tansy's room.

But on the whole, he hadn't minded moving on to greener pastures. Or at least, richer ones. He hoped. Indian Springs wasn't a big town, but the last time he'd been through it had two saloons—with cigars *and* champagne— and a pretty fair whorehouse.

And Becky.

Suddenly, he smiled. Becky. He sure hoped Becky Sawyer was still hanging around Indian Springs, and that she hadn't gone and done anything foolish, like marrying up with some farmer or rancher.

He'd last seen her about three years ago, when she was fresh from the east. Blonde, peach-ripe, and creamycomplected, she'd been nineteen and had come out to the territory to settle her late father's estate.

It had turned out to be a real mess, what with Roy Wheeler having his grubby mitts tangled up in her daddy's business, and Slocum had killed a man and wounded two others before it was over.

He didn't suppose the town of Indian Springs at large would be all that overjoyed to see him back—Roy Wheeler had owned most of it, and the folks had gone lax, what with Wheeler looking out for them. He'd been a benevolent dictator, so to speak, but what the folks hadn't known was what Wheeler had planned for them, once he got hold of the rest of town. Now Wheeler was doing fifteen years in the Territorial Prison at Yuma.

Becky, however, would be another matter.

If she hadn't married.

Or gone back east.

Or entered a goddamn convent.

He snorted. "Fat chance of that," he muttered beneath his breath. If ever there was an unlikely candidate for a life of chastity and poverty (not to mention those other vows, which he had forgotten a long time ago), it was Becky Sawyer.

Yessir, Becky Sawyer at Indian Springs.

Why the hell hadn't he thought of that a couple of weeks ago? Well, he'd just circle around town and go straight on out to her daddy's ranch. Her ranch, now: the Bar S.

He urged Concho into a smooth jog, and as he did, he began to whistle.

Rebecca Sawyer Jamison knelt by the grave she had just placed flowers on, paused for a moment of silent prayer, genuflected, then rose again.

She had cast aside her mourning black months ago, although she still deeply missed Jack. She hadn't loved him, not really, and she supposed that he hadn't loved her. But he had been an anchor for her, someone to lean on, and someone to oversee her business affairs—and broaden them—once Slocum had ridden off into the sunset.

Damn that Slocum anyway!

Jack had been good to her. Always polite, always thanked her for the few meals she herself concocted, and remarked on how good they were, even when she knew they weren't. Which was most of the time. She'd always been a poor excuse for a cook.

Jack had been terribly sweet, she'd give him that: a widower, gray-haired and mustachioed, tall and sinewy with a ready laugh, and he'd owned the ranch that bordered the Bar S to the north. He'd been a friend of her father's, too.

She brushed dust from her skirts. "I could have done a lot worse than you, Jack Jamison," she whispered to his headstone. "Yes, a whole lot worse."

Turning, she walked back toward the ranch house. She had moved from the Bar S and into the Cross J with Jack, and they had combined the two ranches to create a new, much larger one with a new brand: the S Bar J. These days, there was a skeleton crew staying over at the old Bar S's bunkhouse to mind the stock, greet what few visitors came there, and oversee Becky's flock of milk goats, but that was about it.

The S Bar J was an entirely different matter, however. The house was twice as big as the one at the Bar S, and the outbuildings far more numerous. Jack Jamison had been successful, far more successful than her daddy, bless his dear old soul, had ever dreamt of being.

Becky was a rich woman now—or at least better off than most—although she didn't know how much longer that would last. When Slocum had come, he'd gotten rid of Roy Wheeler for her, all right—and, in the process, ruined her for any other man, damn his eyes. But a newer, bigger fish had stepped in to take Roy Wheeler's place.

Tate McMahon.

Just the thought of his name sent shivers of dread and loathing through her.

She would not marry Tate McMahon, no matter how many times he asked, no matter how many times he begged, no matter how many times he demanded it. She had a feeling that the time for asking and begging—and demanding—would be done with shortly, though. Next time, or the one after that, or the one after that, he'd ride out towing his damned pet judge and wed her at gunpoint.

He'd threatened it. Just like he'd threatened Jack's life.

And now Jack was gone.

"Miss Becky?" said a soft voice at her elbow.

Becky had trudged all the way from the grave, around the house, and to the front porch without realizing it.

She turned toward the intrusive voice. "Yes, Tia Juanita?"

The round Mexican housekeeper smiled softly, dimples sinking into her chubby cheeks, and lifted the thin shawl from Becky's shoulders. "And how was Mr. Jamison today?" she asked.

"Same as usual," Becky said with a tired sigh. "Still dead."

Tia Juanita shook her head. She had come with Becky from her father's ranch, having been his servant of long standing. She wasn't anybody's aunt that Becky knew of, but everybody called her Tia—or "aunt"—Juanita.

Even Jack had.

Even Slocum had.

Stop it! she told herself. *Just stop thinking about some man who's long gone! What's got into you lately, anyway?*

She had known he wasn't coming back. She'd known it since the first time she'd seen him. He was a wanderer, a nomad, and with him, everything had to be taken day by day.

Which was the exact opposite of Jack. With Jack, everything was forever. Once Jack moved a piece of furniture into the house, you knew it was going to stay in exactly the same place until hell froze over. You didn't like it so much—it was like beef and beans compared to candy and cake—but it was nourishing. And she had thought that it—and Jack—would be there forever. After all, he was too damned stubborn to die.

Slocum, she figured, had been all frosting and sweet insofar as loving went. Mighty fine when you had it, but a brief treat. You couldn't live on it. Not forever.

It had turned out you couldn't live too long or well on Jack's kind of love, either.

Not when there was somebody lurking out there with a long-range rifle.

Tia Juanita opened the screened door and ushered her through, into the house. The inside was cooler by about ten degrees than the outside, the walls being made of thick adobe. Jack had built it well, to last forever.

Across the big parlor, which was actually in the same open space as the dining room, stood a large stone fireplace, built from rocks that Jack had collected around the ranch. And over the mantel, all by itself, hung a portrait of the man himself: steely hard, rail-thin, with that gray hair and mustache and those cool eyes, and holding his ever-present Stetson in his hands. He wasn't smiling, but he wasn't mad. The little creases that winged out from the corners of his eyes all but said, "I feel damned stupid sitting for this harebrained portrait, but I'll do it for you, Becky."

The last rays of the afternoon sun slanted in through the western windows, covering the big, dark dining room table with wide stripes of white light, and Becky pulled out a chair. She sat, propped her head in her hands, and asked, "What are we going to do, Tia Juanita?"

The housekeeper, knowing a rhetorical question when she heard one, didn't reply. Instead, she said, "I have enchiladas baking."

"That would be good," Becky said absently.

Slocum made camp just before sunset, in a little gorge about ten miles out of Indian Springs.

As he curried Concho, his thoughts were mostly filled with Becky Sawyer. He'd been musing on her most of the afternoon, and the idea of her was sounding better and better to him all the time.

In his mind, he'd just about decided that she couldn't have gone back east, or married, or any of those other things he'd been thinking about. Not Becky Sawyer. No, she'd be waiting for him with open arms.

He wondered if she still made that good pot roast—and that god-awful gravy.

"Man, that was tough stuff," he said to the horse. Well, this time they'd let that Mexican gal—what was her name? Tia something or other?—do all the cooking. He figured they'd be otherwise occupied.

Giving Concho a last pat on the neck, a smiling Slocum put his curry comb and body brush away, then set off to gather wood for the fire.

3

Tate McMahon peered between the toes of his boots—
which were resting on the polished cherry desk before
him—at the clock.

It was 9:30 in the morning. Another two and a half
hours before he gathered Judge Radnor and a couple of
witnesses (quite a few, actually, and all bearing guns) and
took a little ride out to the Jamison place. Another two
and a half hours until he'd be a married—and very rich—
man.

He smiled.

Through the front window, he watched the panorama
of Main Street. Well, it wouldn't have been much of a
panorama compared to, say, New York City. But out here
in the godforsaken middle of nowhere, it was fairly grand.

Every single place on the street which used to bear the
name of Wheeler now had McMahon emblazoned in its
place. McMahon Dry Goods, the McMahon Livery, Mc-
Mahon Feed and Grain, and the local saloon, the Mc-
Mahon Palace: these were just four such properties he
could see out the front window.

The bank didn't bear his name. That was still the Indian
Springs Bank. But he owned it.

He owned just about everything.

God bless whoever it was that had put Roy Wheeler in jail, that was all he had to say. He had forgotten the name of the man who'd done it, but he gathered it was some sort of saddle bum with a grudge, and he didn't much care. What he did care about was that it had cleared the way for him, and he was eager to fit right in.

He had.

Except that where old, short-sighted Roy Wheeler had failed to sew up the majority of property around town, Tate McMahon had succeeded. After all, he had a more pressing reason to grab it, and grab it fast. Tate McMahon had offered a bit more—and more persistently—than Wheeler had.

Times were changing, and things moved faster. Why, they had a telegraph and a train station right here in town! A man had to be persistent these days if he wanted to get anything done.

And Tate McMahon was nothing if not a persistent man.

Except that nothing had worked on Becky Jamison, absolutely nothing. Not even killing her husband, Jack Jamison. Criminal, really. Why, Jack had been old enough to be her father!

Outside of his land holdings, which had grown considerably since he started scooping up titles and deeds and mortgages like they were going out of style, Becky Jamison held the single largest spread around: the Bar S and the Cross J, which were now combined into the S Bar J.

Once he had that, he'd have a lock-tight hold on Indian Springs, and all the land around it for a good hundred miles in every direction. He needed a hundred miles, if only for a buffer zone between himself and the world.

Again, he stared out the window. There went Homer Dain. Probably going into the feed store to pick up a few more hundred-pound bags of oats. McMahon congratulated himself on having been smart enough to lease back the ranches to the families who had originally owned them. Why, Roy Wheeler had kicked them off their properties!

Stupid, that's what Wheeler had been. Eventually, had Wheeler gotten his way, there would have been no one left in town outside Wheeler himself and his henchmen, and the place would have fair dried up. No one to run the shops, to mind the bank, to do all those little jobs McMahon considered beneath him, no one to buy the doodads that only women bought. No one to keep the economy bubbling along.

He didn't mind that he didn't own the tobacconist or the haberdasher or the gunsmith or any manner of smaller enterprises. He didn't care about them, and he left them in peace. As long as he had his hands in all the major businesses and all the land—and the mineral rights—he would be content.

He wasn't greedy, after all.

He checked the wall clock again. The hands had only moved fifteen minute's worth.

He wondered if Judge Radnor had yet woken from his usual drunken coma. Probably not. Probably not until eleven or so.

Ah, well. He had waited this long to get married; he could wait a little longer. He wondered if there was a piano out at the S Bar J. He couldn't remember. He hoped there was, though. Music would be nice. It made things more . . . official.

He smiled. "Da, da, duh-dum," he began to sing softly.

Slocum was in a pretty good mood when he jogged Concho into the yard at the Bar S Ranch at along about eleven that morning. He rode through a flock of bleating goats, which seemed to be milling all over the yard, made his way up to the porch, dismounted, and gave Concho a jovial pat on the neck.

Wearing a giant-sized grin, he threw his reins around the hitching rail and went on up to the front door.

But when he knocked, it wasn't opened by Tia What's-her-name, as he had expected. Instead, it was answered by a lone, rangy cowhand wearing nothing but his long johns, his boots, his hat, and a red-checkered napkin tucked high under his chin.

Furthermore, he was holding a fried chicken leg and was looking just a touch annoyed—to have been disturbed during his late breakfast, Slocum figured. Or early lunch.

The hand didn't look half as annoyed as Slocum felt, though. His anticipatory grin had long since evaporated.

"Mornin', friend," the hand drawled lazily, and took a bite of chicken. Through a mouthful of half-masticated meat, he said, "Can I help you with somethin' or other?"

Slocum clenched his hands into fists, but didn't raise them. If Becky had sunk so low as to take this good-for-nothing cowpoke to her bed, well, she could have him and he could have her.

But he said, "Becky Sawyer around?"

The cowpoke scratched his head. "You ain't seen her for a while, have you, Mister?"

Slocum didn't reply.

His silence didn't faze the cowpoke, though. "Because Miss Becky up and got herself wed 'bout two years back," he continued. "Well, now that I come to think about it, it might have been two and a half. Moved up the road to the Cross J," he went on lazily, pointing toward the north with his drumstick while he held the screen door wide with the other hand.

"Used to be the Cross J, that is," he went on. "Course, it's the S Bar J, now." From horizon to horizon, he swept out the arm with the half-eaten chicken leg in it, nearly poking Slocum in the nose, which didn't make him any happier about the situation. "All this is," the cowhand said.

"Is what?" Slocum asked tersely.

The cowpoke swallowed another bite of chicken. "The S Bar J, what'd you think? See now, Mr. Jack Jamison, he was the Cross J, and Miss Sawyer, her papa was the Bar S. Course, that was a long time before I come to work here. Anyways, when she——"

Slocum waved his hands in the air, cutting the underwear-clad cowhand off. "I got that part," he said. "Becky Sawyer got married?" Frankly, he was a little shocked.

And pissed.

"Yup," the man said, and tossed his chicken bone to the side of the porch, where it was snatched up by a waiting barn cat, who ran under the bushes with it.

The cowhand wiped the greasy fingers of his free hand on his front, which, by the looks of it, had been serving as a hand-wipe for a week or two.

"Course, she's widowed now," he went on lackadaisically. "Real shame 'bout Mr. Jamison, a real shame. Never was a more fair boss or a better human bein' on the face of this here earth. Yessir, a real shame."

Slocum let out a long sigh. Becky had been married and widowed in less than thirty seconds—well, it seemed that way to him, anyhow—but he still had no idea where she was except a general direction: north.

He looked the cowpoke square in the eye and growled, "I'm only gonna ask you this one more time, and you can either answer me in the shortest way possible, or else you can end up in that horse trough over there with that chicken leg stuck up your butt. Crosswise. *Comprende?*"

The perplexed cowpoke blinked rapidly, then nodded his head.

"Where is Becky?" Slocum said, overpronouncing every word.

Now it was he who held up one hand against the screen door. He leaned forward menacingly, and the cowboy snatched his hand away.

"T-told you, M-mister," the cowpoke stuttered. "Straight up the north road, at the S Bar J. She lives there n-now."

Slocum took a step backward and let the screen door slam closed between them. The startled cowhand hopped back a good foot.

"Go back to your goddamned chicken," Slocum said as he climbed down the porch steps.

Slocum jogged Concho up the rutted dirt path that passed for a road, and which was supposed to lead to the S Bar J.

After some thought, he had remembered Jack Jamison. He'd only met him once. He recalled a tallish, wiry man, gray-haired, lean, and with a thick mustache. He'd seemed a nice enough fellow, but was far too old for someone like Becky.

Of course, Slocum was, too, but at least he wasn't old enough to be her goddamn grandfather, which the Jack Jamison he remembered had been.

But she'd married the old coot, hadn't she? And now he'd died.

He wished he'd stuck around to get a little more information. For instance, exactly when Jamison had died.

And how.

As much as he'd stirred himself up about seeing Becky again—and doing a few things with her, too—he didn't want to burst in on her while she was still wearing a veil and mourning black. Or weeping buckets over a lost husband.

He whoaed up Concho and sat for a moment in the thin purple shade of a giant palo verde, right at the crossroads to town, and considered the possibilities of the situation.

No, it wouldn't be the right thing for him to just ride up there big as life, expecting her to just welcome him with open arms, let alone open legs.

Mayhap he'd be better off to ride toward town and settle into a poker game. Have himself a cigar or two. That's what he'd wanted in the first place, before he'd remembered Becky, wasn't it?

And he could have a different woman every night, a string of nice, anonymous, big-breasted women he paid for.

It would sure be safer.

But then again, he'd never been the sort for "safe," and he supposed he should pay his respects. Why, if Becky heard that he'd been in town and hadn't come by, she'd probably be awful mad! Or awful disappointed.

Or awful something.

Then again, it might be awful embarrassing to go out there and find her swathed in black. Or still pissed at him for riding out and leaving her with no alternative but to marry Jack Jamison. . . .

He wondered if she'd loved him.

He reined Concho east, toward town, and rode about twenty feet.

"Aw, hell," he said, turning the horse back toward the road north. The lure of Becky Sawyer Jamison was stronger than the lure of champagne and cigars could ever be. Even if she was holding a grudge or mourning like nobody's business.

"I might's well just stop in to pay my respects," he muttered to Concho. "Bein' as I'm this close and all . . ."

4

A little before noon, just as she was sitting down to a lunch of leftover enchiladas and rice, Becky heard a ruckus outside.

"Tia Juanita?" she called, but when there was no answer she went to the door herself.

Wiping her hands on her checkered napkin, she opened the door, expecting one of the hands, perhaps Dave or Pete.

Instead, she saw Tate McMahon on the porch, and he was grinning at her. There were several armed men with him, two of which stood over beside the corral, holding the struggling Pete's arms.

"Tate," she said flatly. "Let Pete go."

Tate McMahon grinned. It was a decidedly unwholesome smile. A waste of human flesh, Becky thought. Tate McMahon would have been a nice-looking fellow if he'd been anybody but Tate McMahon. As he was, he made her skin crawl.

He lifted a hand, and the two men holding Pete suddenly set him free. The force of Pete's struggle—and sudden release—took him a few feet forward, and his hand automatically went toward his hip. But Becky shook her head and gestured to him before he could do anything silly, like draw his gun.

Instead, he picked up his hat from the dust and slapped his thigh with it in frustration. Blond, green-eyed and rangy, Pete was a good man, even if he wasn't exactly first in line when the Lord was handing out brains. But he'd been with her daddy for ten years before she came back from the east, and he was as loyal as they came.

She didn't want to be responsible for his death, and judging by the odds, letting him pull that gun would have been the same as killing him herself.

Just as she heard Tia Juanita's familiar footsteps behind her, she saw the little surprise Tate had brought along: Judge Harry P. Radnor, still recuperating from last night's drunk from the look of it, slouched behind him. Rumpled, pale, and slightly green, he clung, wavering and weaving, to the porch rail.

She stared straight up into Tate's blue eyes. She had always liked blue eyes before, but now she was beginning to detest them. Tate McMahon's were pale, ghostly, and cold as ice.

"Go back home, to town," she said, and swung the door closed.

But he stuck his arm out and braced it open. "Not today, darlin'." The grin on his face was absolutely maddening. "Why do you want to go and be so mulish on your wedding day?"

Becky drew herself up. She was scared, but she'd be damned if she'd let him know it.

"Wedding day, my aunt Fanny!" she said. "Get out of here, Tate McMahon. You may own practically everything else around, but you don't own the S Bar J. You're trespassing."

"Not for long, Becky, honey," he said. His smile never wavered, damn him. "Not for more than a couple of minutes. Judge?"

Judge Radnor, all five-foot-six of him, stepped forward tentatively, and tugged his dirty vest down over his protruding belly. "Yes, Mr. McMahon?" he slurred. "Is the blushing bride ready?"

Becky felt herself pushed aside, and Tia Juanita stepped in front of her, planting her sizable bulk between Becky and McMahon. She brandished an iron skillet, the great big one she used for frying two chickens at a time.

"You do what Mrs. Jamison says, Mr. McMahon," she said, pounding the skillet against the flat of her hand. "If she says that you are not welcome here, then you are not welcome. And you take this drunken old fool with you."

She threw a piercing glance toward Judge Radnor. *"Borracho!"* she sneered, then spat upon the floor. "You are a disgrace to both the law and the Territory."

Tate's smile wavered, and he reached out, toward Tia Juanita's throat. But Tia Juanita was quicker. She thrust the iron skillet upward so that his fingers jammed into it, and he yelped.

Suddenly, Becky heard Pete laugh. But it was suddenly cut off when one of Tate's men clubbed him over the head with the butt of a gun. All around, hands went toward guns before Tate could get his bruised fingers to his mouth.

And then a new voice broke the silence.

"Why, Becky Sawyer!" it said. "Ain't seen you for a coon's age!"

She had no idea how he'd gotten there, but the voice was unmistakable: Slocum.

Her Slocum, come back, and at just exactly the right moment. She didn't know whether to cheer him on or slap him.

She turned toward the sound, and this time it was she who pushed Tia Juanita aside.

There he was in the rugged flesh, all six-feet-one of him, dark-haired and green-eyed, and not looking a bit changed from the last time she'd seen him. Suddenly mindless of the impending danger that was all around her in the form of Tate McMahon's men, she ran out onto the porch, down its length, and threw herself into Slocum's arms.

"How did you get here?" she whispered into his ear. "How did you know?" She glanced around, looking for something and not finding it. "And where on earth is your horse?"

"I'm no wizard, honey," he whispered back before he lifted her, moving her brusquely to one side. "Looks like you got yourself a little problem here," he said as he stepped in front of her, shielding her body with his. She let him.

She also noticed that several of McMahon's minions were whispering among themselves, and a few of them backed off. They looked frightened.

Another man simply stared at Slocum, his mouth open.

But Tate McMahon, blast his sanctimonious hide, held steady. "Slocum," he said. "That sounds vaguely familiar." He rubbed the back of his neck while one of his men whispered something in his ear, and then he brightened.

"Would you be the same Slocum who put Roy Wheeler in prison?"

"Depends on which Slocum you're meanin'," Slocum answered smoothly. He pointed toward Pete. "And you'd best pray that cowhand your boy just buffaloed is all right. He's a friend of mine." Becky wished she could see Slocum's face.

"Oh, I think you're him, all right," Tate replied, answering his own question. "I've heard something about you. You looking for a job? I could use a gun like you."

Becky made a little growling sound in her throat and moved to the side to go around Slocum. Her hands were balled into fists, and she was ready and willing—if less than able—to smash Tate McMahon's nose in all by her lonesome.

But Slocum swung out his left arm, easily—and maddeningly—holding her still, and said, "Sorry, buddy. I've already got myself a job."

Tate cocked his head. "Don't tell me you're working for my fiancé, here!"

"I am *not* your—" Becky started, but Slocum held her back.

And before Slocum could form one of his patented maddening sarcastic replies, Tia Juanita said, "Your noon meal will be on the table, Slocum. As soon as we rid ourselves of this uninvited company, that is. And Pete is moving, Miss Becky. I can see him."

"Thank you, Tia Juanita," Becky chirped over Slocum's arm.

At five-feet-four, she just came up to his shoulder. How had he known she was in trouble? Or had he known at all?

It didn't matter. He had thrown himself directly into the thick of it, now.

He was wonderful. He was stupendous! He was so . . . infuriating!

"Have we concluded our business, Mr. McMahon?" Becky said.

"Why now, I never thought of a wedding as 'business,' darlin'," he purred. She wanted to slap him or slug him, or at least flatten him with a shovel. "And what's this with this 'Mister' business all of a sudden?"

"Go home, Tate," she said through gritted teeth. "Now." She glanced out into the yard, and saw that Pete was, indeed, beginning to stir. Thank God he wasn't hurt badly!

McMahon looked out over his men, and Becky guessed that even he could see that they all appeared a little jumpy.

Becky hoped that he'd also decide that discretion was the better part of valor.

He did, thank Heaven.

He tipped his hat to her. "We'll finish this another time, then, Becky," he said. Pulling the confused judge by his coat sleeve, he went down the steps and mounted his horse. His men followed his example, although quite a bit more nervously, she noticed. Their heads were twisting like owls.

Then McMahon touched the brim of his hat and nodded toward her savior. "Slocum," he said. "Ladies."

He rode on out of the yard, he and his men raising a low roil of dust behind them.

Slocum turned to face her. "Howdy, Becky," he said. "You want to tell me what that marriage crap was all about?"

Instead of kissing him square on the mouth, she hauled off and slapped his face just as hard as she could, then stalked off into the house.

The slam of the door ringing in her ears, she fled through the main rooms. As she ran down the long hall her tears suddenly spilled over, and she threw herself on her bed, sobbing.

Damn that Slocum, anyway!

5

Slocum stood on the porch, one hand to his stinging cheek, staring after Becky. "What was that for?" he demanded of Tia Juanita.

The housekeeper shrugged her shoulders. "Bad mood, maybe?"

"Plumb loco, more like," Slocum growled as he yanked open the screen and walked past her, into the house. Becky had disappeared into the back someplace, and after he had a moment to think about it, he figured that right now wouldn't exactly be the time to go and fetch her. Not if he didn't want his face smacked again.

Women!

Besides, Tia Juanita was already guiding him toward a dining room chair. The big oak table was set for one, but she quickly whisked away the plate of enchiladas before he could launch himself at it.

"It is cold," she said, wagging a finger. "I will make you a new plate. And then, if Becky has not come out from her room, we will talk."

"At least somebody's talkin' to me," Slocum grumbled. He took off his sweat-stained hat and tossed it across the

31

table, where it hooked over the backrest of a chair, twirled twice, then came to rest.

Behind him, the screen door banged once again, and he twisted toward it.

Immediately, he rose and stepped forward, hand out. "Pete!" he said. "Glad to see you! How's that head a'yours?"

The big blond man gripped his hand with equal enthusiasm and shook it vigorously. "Never thought we'd see the likes of you again, you old dog. Oh, my head's fine. It's took worse hits than that. My ol' daddy used to say it was thicker'n a two by four, anyhow. How you been, you ol' brush popper?"

Both men pulled out chairs at the table and sat down.

"Pretty good," admitted Slocum, "right up until about five minutes ago. What the hell's goin' on with Becky? And who were those fellers?"

"Hold on a second," Pete said, his face screwed up. "You mean you didn't hear nothin'? 'Bout Miss Becky, I mean."

"Hear what?"

Pete took off his hat and began feeling his scalp for a bump. "I'll have to start puttin' more cash into the collection plate come next Sunday," he said, wincing when he found one. "The Lord surely does work in mysterious ways, all right."

Slocum hooked his elbow over the back of his chair. "You wanna start talkin' American, Pete?"

From the front door, somebody called, "Hey, Pete? Who's this nice Appaloosa belong to? Found him tied to the back of the house, and—"

"He's mine," Slocum hollered. "That Dave Shepherd I hear out there?"

The screen door creaked open and a head, curly with red hair, peeked in, then lit up. "By God!" he said. "Slocum?"

"Get your lazy ass in here, Dave," Pete called, still feeling his head.

Slocum started to rise. "I'd best tend my horse," he said. "And you'd better get a cold compress on your noggin, buddy. That's startin' to swell."

But Pete put a hand on his shoulder. "Set back down. Dave'll get somebody to see to your horse. You still ridin' a Palouse horse?"

"Nothin' but," replied Slocum as he sat again. Outside, he heard Dave hollering toward the barn. Slocum asked Pete, "Where were all these hands when Becky was in trouble out there?"

Pete shrugged. "Hidin' in the barn, probably." He turned toward the kitchen. "Hey, Tia Juanita! Can I have somethin' cold for my head?"

A salty grumbling issued from the kitchen, but that was all. Pete seemed unnerved by it, though, and turned back to Slocum.

"Dave was up checkin' the north pasture, though, or he would'a been right out there with me, gettin' himself buffaloed like a blame fool," he said. "You can't blame them boys for hidin', Slocum. Most folks round these parts are plumb scared of Tate McMahon. Least, the ranchers are. He holds most of the paper on the property around Indian Springs."

Tia Juanita stepped from the kitchen, a steaming plate in her hand. She slid it in front of Slocum, handed a folded, damp cloth to Pete, indicating he was to put in on his head, and said, "Was one, is now two. You invite anybody else, Pete?"

"Dave, I reckon," Pete replied with a grin. "Gonna take at least two of us to bring old Slocum up to date."

"Three for dinner!" the housekeeper grumbled. "All right. I suppose you will save me the trouble of explaining. But you men, you take your spurs off right now. You will not scratch my floors!"

•   •   •

While Pete and Dave were busy enlightening Slocum—
and swallowing a surplus of goat cheese–covered enchiladas, beans, and rice and washing it down with limeade
by the pitcherful—Tia Juanita carried a tray back to
Becky Jamison's bedroom. She stood in the hall and
shifted the tray to one hand, hesitated slightly, then softly
rapped.

"I brought you lunch, little one," she said. "May I come
in?"

The door cracked open and one of Becky's tear-swollen
eyes appeared. "Sure," she said, and sniffled. "Come on
in."

Tia Juanita carried the tray to the window and slid it
onto the top of a low desk, then turned toward Becky and
folded her arms.

Becky wiped her nose and, with the familiarity that
comes from time and shared secrets, said, "Why can't you
just be like a servant?"

"Because I know you too well, my Becky. And your
papa." The housekeeper shook her head. "Why did you
slap Slocum? I know there must be some bad feelings,
but you were just about to have to take Mr. McMahon as
your husband. I think Slocum showing up is a very good
thing, no?"

Becky gave her nose a last wipe, then stuck the handkerchief down into her skirt pocket with a sharp, jabbing
motion. She crossed the room and sat down at the desk,
then lifted the napkin from the tray.

"When are you going to learn to cook American?" she
muttered.

"You don't like it, you should cook more often," Tia
Juanita said stubbornly, arms still crossed. "My cooking
was good enough for your papa, and good enough for you
for the past three years! And you are changing the sub-
ject."

The knife and fork in Becky's hands sagged down to the desk top. "I don't know why I did it, Tia Juanita. I mean, his showing up, just at that moment? It was like a . . . like a miracle or something."

Tia Juanita said nothing, but genuflected, an action that Becky, staring blankly at her plate of enchiladas, did not see. Tia Juanita had been praying for just such a thing without cease since the death of Jack Jamison. "So you strike him because he is sent from God?"

Becky ignored her facetious tone. "It was just," Becky continued, "that once I actually saw him I remembered the way he lit out last time, and . . . hell, I know that's not reason enough. I know I should be grateful. I mean, he got rid of Roy Wheeler for us, didn't he?"

"And now, with God's help, he will make Mr. McMahon go away," replied Tia Juanita, adding gently, "and you always knew he would go, little one."

Becky turned in her chair and cocked her head. She had always been a sweet thing, one that Tia Juanita would have been proud to call her own daughter. That was, had Becky Sawyer Jamison possessed the sense to be born a Mexican, and not in some far-flung, foreign place called Massachusetts.

At last, with a sniffle, Becky said, "Did you find out how . . . how he knew to come? How he knew I was in trouble?"

"He did not know," replied Tia Juanita. "He just came." She did not add that she was certain Slocum had come directly because of her prayers. Of course, she hadn't mentioned Slocum specifically, but then, the Lord worked in His own time and in His own way. She would not question it.

She picked up the napkin and dropped it into Becky's lap. "Now, cry the last of those tears and eat your dinner, little one. And then you will wash out your pretty eyes and come greet your guest in a more fitting manner."

•   •   •

Slocum leaned back and tossed his napkin on the table.
It had been a good meal.

He dug into his pocket and pulled out his fixings pouch
as he said, "So how come you figure this McMahon
turned tail, Dave? Can't see as how I outnumbered him.
By much."

Pete snorted and Dave grinned.

Dave said, "Well, I reckon they lit out for the same
reason you been tellin' us all them dandies has been callin' you out."

Pete nodded. "Whatever rumor got them fellers goin'
is catchin'. Looks like we got it here, too. Least, that's
how I see it."

"Yup," said Dave. " 'Cept none of them fellers had the
guts to try'n snooker you into skinnin' that smokewagon."

Slocum licked his quirlie a last time and stuck it between his lips. "Wish I knew who the hell started this
whole thing," he said as he pulled out a lucifer and struck
it into flame. "Like to pop him one upside the jaw," he
continued. "I mean, I'm sort'a used to some'a that shit,
but this is too much. Gets on a feller's nerves."

"Likely," Pete interjected, "that rumor started out a
whole lot different than what's gettin' passed around by
this time." With a thumb, he tamped his pipe. "It's like
that game we used to play when we was kids. You remember, Dave?"

"I do," Dave said, nodding. Dave and Pete had grown
up together back in Kansas, as Slocum recalled. "The one
where you got in a line and started whisperin' down it?"

Pete struck a match and nodded. "And what started out
as 'Bob's got him a new pup' ended up as—"

"—'A mad dog killed Bob with an axe,' " Slocum
quipped, even though he didn't feel much like laughing.
He took a long drag on his smoke while Dave brayed and
slapped his knee.

Pete, chuckling, lit that old carved bulldog Meershaum of his.

"Well," said Pete, puffing smoke, "all's I know is Tate McMahon's two times as bad as your old friend Roy Wheeler ever was. And I, for one, was plumb glad to see him ridin' out of here this morning."

"Amen," said Dave.

"Aw, you didn't see nothin', Dave," muttered Pete.

Grouchily, Dave replied, "Well, you know what I mean."

Suddenly, Slocum stood up.

"What the hell you doin', Slocum?" asked Dave.

Slocum ignored him. "Afternoon, Becky," he said carefully. He wasn't about to coax her into flying off the handle again.

The other two men belatedly scraped their chairs back and stood, also.

"Miz Jamison, ma'am," they said, as one.

She waved them back down into their seats. Slocum remained on his feet, though.

She looked beautiful, despite the fact that she'd obviously been crying. Her face was heart-shaped, her lips lush and naturally deep pink. Her eyes were huge, round, deep blue, and lushly fringed with sooty lashes. Fine, arched brows the color of smoke rode over them.

She was of moderate height, with hair the color of sweet clover honey and skin like pale, tawny silk—skin that Slocum longed to touch. Firm, round breasts rode above a tiny waist which belled into round hips tapering into coltish legs.

That was as he remembered.

He found himself wanting to see those legs again in the worst way.

Not to mention the rest of her.

"Care to walk with me, Becky?" he asked.

She crossed to the table and plucked his hat from its

hook on the chair. She turned it over in her hands, studying it, then abruptly tossed it to him over Pete and Dave.

They both ducked, but she paid them no mind and said, "I'd be pleased, Slocum."

6

They walked out toward the main corral where several horses lazed, Concho among them. Slocum respected Becky's silence and said nothing until they came to a stop beside the fence, between two towering cottonwood trees. Swishing flies, Concho began to lazily wander over.

Slocum placed a hand on each of Becky's shoulders, sighed deeply, and said, "What the hell's goin' on, darlin'?"

She looked at the ground, and Slocum half-expected her to dig her toe into the ground. She didn't though. She said, "I'm sorry, Slocum. For hitting you, I mean. It's just . . . just . . ."

And then suddenly she moved forward, threw her arms around his waist, and began to sob: big, deep, heaving sobs that seemed to well up from her toes and gain strength as they moved up and out.

Slocum, at a loss, simply held her.

She clung to him for a good five minutes, until she seemed to be all cried out, and then she started to hiccup.

Holding back a smile, he reached into his pocket and brought out a fresh bandana, which he wedged between her moist, jolting face and his chest.

39

"Here," he said softly. "Dry those eyes and blow your nose."

She obeyed, letting out a most unladylike honk. This time, he couldn't help but let his mouth quirk up just a little. Such a big snort to come from such a little gal!

She looked up, hiccuping and blushing, and smiling just a little. "Never was especially ladylike, I'm afraid," she said.

"But you always were all woman," he replied, and taking the bandana, wiped away a tear she had missed. "You ready to talk yet? Or would you rather take another swing at me?"

When Becky cringed with embarrassment, he added, "Hey, I'm a strappin' fella, honey. I think I can handle it."

She turned away and braced herself, her elbows splayed on the top rail of the corral fence, the shade from the cottonwoods dappling her shoulders. "I may take you up on that later," she said softly. He couldn't see her face.

"What is it, Becky? And why is that Tate McMahon buying up everything in sight? Roy Wheeler, I could figure. He kicked those families off. Wanted the rangeland. But McMahon?" He scratched the back of his head. "Dave and Pete tell me he's not doing a damned thing with those properties, even rents 'em back to the families he stole them off of." He snorted. "I don't get it."

She turned to face him. "I don't either. It doesn't make any sense. But that doesn't change the fact that he's still trying to own this whole valley. I'm the last holdout, Slocum. I'm sure he had Jack murdered because he wouldn't sell. And when it turned out that I wouldn't, either, well . . . you saw what he was up to today. I've been expecting it. Just not so soon, that's all."

She paused, then added more softly, "They told you about Jack, didn't they?"

Slocum nodded. "They did. I'm right sorry for your

loss, Becky. I recall meeting him. He was a fine man."

He didn't add that he thought Jack Jamison was far too old for a young gal in her prime, even if the sonofabitch washed his neck and knew his table manners. She likely didn't want to hear it.

Besides, it was none of his business.

"Yes," she said. "He was. He was a very good man."

She paused again, but when she spoke anew, it wasn't about Jack Jamison. "Why did you come?" she asked.

What could he tell her? That he'd been riding along aimlessly and remembered her as a nice, convenient piece of tail? Hell, that wouldn't do at all!

So he said, "I was close—just down to Bedrock—and thought I'd stop in to pay my respects, that's all. See how you were doing." He shrugged. "Comin' in when I did, well, that was just dumb luck. Lucky for you, anyhow."

With his thumb, he raised her chin until she was looking into his eyes. He smiled down at her. "I'd have hated to show up and find out you'd been wed not once, but twice since I last saw you." The smile faded. "Besides, it'd pain me something terrible to have to put your new bridegroom in jail."

"You think he's up to something, too, don't you, Slocum? I mean something more than it looks like." She blinked, fluttering long, sooty lashes over tear-stained eyes. "And you're going to do something about it?"

"Oh, I think he's definitely up to somethin' real rotten, honey. Somethin' besides tryin' to steal all the land around Indian Springs and railroad you into a wedding, I mean. As if that wasn't bad enough." He smiled again, and when she returned it, he brushed a kiss over her forehead.

"And yes," he added softly, "I'm gonna do something about it."

Hell, he figured he was sort of *stuck* with doing something about it, now!

"Thank you, Slocum," Becky whispered. "Thank you for everything."

"Don't thank me, honey," he said, chuckling. "I haven't done anything yet."

"Yes, you have. You came. And you were so . . . so nice about poor Jack." She sniffed again, and tears threatened to spill from her eyes.

"Suck those tears back in, gal," he said. "I told you, I just came because I was passin' this way. And I have no right to get upset 'cause you married Jack Jamison. I think . . . I think you made a good match," he added, lying through his teeth.

That did it. She launched into a new wave of tears.

Slocum could do nothing but hold her.

Dave and Pete vied for a place at the front window.

"There!" hissed Dave. "Is he kissin' her?"

Pete elbowed him out of the way. "No, you piece'a cow dung. Only her forehead."

"Well, hell!" exclaimed Dave, rubbing his rib cage. "That counts, don't it?"

Pete rolled his eyes. "Not hardly."

Tia Juanita, who had been standing in the kitchen doorway, rolled her eyes.

"Enough!" she announced, stepping forward. She took both cowhands, each by an arm, and led them back into the depths of the house and away from the window.

"For shame," she said, shaking her finger at them. "Grown men, spying like children."

Pete, at least, had the good sense to look embarrassed. "We were just seein' whether it was safe to go outside yet," he said. "We didn't want to bother 'em. You know, in case they had something goin' on like last time."

"Sit," Tia Juanita demanded, pointing to two chairs.

"On the parlor furniture?" Dave asked, both eyebrows hiked.

"Sit," repeated Tia Juanita. And when both men had taken careful seats on the edges of the parlor chairs, she announced, "I will tell you when you can go back outside."

She took up their vacated post at the window, and smiling softly, once again crossed herself. It was a godsend to have a real honest-to-goodness man on the place once again.

Especially when that man was Slocum.

Tate McMahon let himself into his office in town and slumped down in the chair behind the desk. He tossed his hat toward the rack, but it hit the wall instead, and slid to the floor.

"Goddamn it," he grumbled, and then picked up a book and threw it just as hard as he could. It banged off the wall with a resounding, if not comforting, *thump*.

Why had this had to happen, today of all days?

Where in the hell had this Slocum character come from?

Oh, he'd been regaled with more than enough Slocum stories on the ride back to town, once his crew had gotten over their cowardice enough to start in jabbering.

His crew. That was a laugh! He ought to fire them all and start over, stock the place with shootists and quick-draw artists and men who knew how to do more than threaten a few cow-poor ranchers, that's what he should do.

On the way back from the S Bar J, he'd heard the story about Slocum and the Confederate camp, Slocum and the taking of Red Morgan, and Slocum taking those crooked mining magnates up in the Dakotas. He didn't mind admitting that that story in particular had given him some pause, until he realized that Cliff Tobin had it on the good word of his cousin who heard it from his brother-in-law, who'd heard it from a fellow who's uncle had been there.

Hmph.

All the stories—those and the dozen others he'd been told in the last hour—were like that. Nobody had ever seen this Slocum do anything, at least, not personally. They just all knew stories passed down third- or fourth-hand.

Stories that had likely grown quite a bit in the telling and retelling.

Oh, he figured that Slocum must have done something, all right. For one thing, he had it on good authority that Slocum had been the fellow who put Roy Wheeler in prison.

He owed Slocum for that, in some sort of lopsided way, he supposed.

But Wheeler had been a stupid fool, and McMahon surely hadn't asked Slocum to come down on Wheeler. That was before McMahon's time in Indian Springs, and Slocum had taken care of Wheeler all by himself. In fact, insofar as McMahon knew, the only thing that Slocum had ever done for certain was to put Roy Wheeler in prison.

Why? McMahon had no idea. And frankly, he didn't care. He was a man set on the future, not the past, and the future had suddenly gotten a hell of a lot more complicated.

He drummed his fingers on the desktop, and it echoed through the empty office. It was Sunday, and he was the only person in the place. Not that there was anyone there—besides Siddons, that was—the rest of the time.

McMahon had made it his business to keep the true nature of what he did—and what he had planned—a secret, even from Siddons.

Siddons didn't seem to mind. She just seemed happy to have the work, which consisted mostly of light filing, a few letters to write and mail—she did have very nice handwriting, he'd say that for her—and running his personal errands.

He had the feeling that if Siddons had known what he was up to with Mrs. Becky Jamison, she would not have been quite so happy in her work. He figured that Siddons had a bit of a secret crush on him. At least, she thought it was secret.

But he'd seen her fluttering her eyelashes and swashing that big, fat ass of hers, and he'd noticed the way she poked her gigantic bosom in his face whenever possible.

But all in all, the charms of an overfed heifer of a secretary faded away to less than nothing in comparison to those of Becky Jamison. Especially when you took Becky's land holdings into account.

Damn that Slocum anyway!

He supposed he should send some wires. He'd been thinking about it all the way in from the S Bar J. Well, once he'd tuned the noise from those gossiping hands out of his head. He'd send for Drug Cassidy, that's what he'd do.

Then they'd all see just how long this trumped-up mankiller of a Slocum character lasted, he thought with a snort.

He pulled out pen and paper and began to compose a brief telegram, then paused.

Perhaps he'd best send for two, he decided. Maybe that Teddy LeGrande fellow. He was supposed to be awfully good. And fast. Almost as fast as Drug Cassidy, they said. LeGrande headquartered in Santa Fe, didn't he?

One nice thing about hiring outsiders, particularly hired guns: they did their job, you gave them money, and then they went away for good. Just like when he'd had Jack Jamison killed. He'd never hear from that old boy—or his killer—again, he thought, and then he laughed out loud.

He composed a second telegram, snatched up his hat, and let himself out of his office. He was actually whistling by then, thinking about what a nice little surprise Slocum was going to have coming.

The nerve of that sonofabitch saddle tramp!

Nobody broke up his wedding day and lived to crow about it!

7

Slocum held her, then listened, then held her some more while her tears soaked through his shirt. When Concho nuzzled him over the corral fence, he gently chucked the horse under his chin before he brushed the hair back from Becky's temple, kissing it gently.

"C'mon, darlin'," he said. "Let's go in the house." He slid his arm around her shoulders, gave a last rub to Concho's forehead, and led Becky, sniffling, across the yard.

A few pecking, red- and white-speckled hens fled at their footsteps, and from inside the house, he could hear the scuffle of boots and the ringing of spurs. He grinned to himself. Tia Juanita had probably given Pete and Dave the go-ahead to walk out across the yard.

He was right. When he opened the front door and ushered Becky inside, he found Tia Juanita standing just inside the window, arms crossed over her considerable bosom, watching while Pete and Dave hurriedly strapped on their spurs again.

Pete looked up from his boot and immediately flushed. "Uh, howdy, folks," he said. "Everything all right?"

And then he flushed even deeper and looked right down at his boots again, fumbling with the spur strap's buckle.

"Just fine," Slocum said, trying not to smile. "You boys leavin' so soon?"

Dave stood all the way up. "We sure are, Slocum," he said, looking even more ill-at-ease than Pete, if that were possible. "Yessirree Bob, we sure are."

He tugged the fabric at Pete's shoulder. "Ain't we, Pete?"

Pete finally got his buckle fastened and grumbled, "Just hold your goddamn horses, Dave," as he got to his feet.

From beneath Slocum's arm, a puzzled Becky piped up, "What on earth is the matter with you boys?"

Slocum squeezed her shoulders.

"Shoo!" said Tia Juanita to Pete and Dave, and pointed toward the door. "Have you lazy *muchachos* nothing else to do with your time?"

"But we was only—" Dave began.

Pete poked him in the ribs, cutting him off, then grabbed both of their hats. He handed Dave's to him, then dragged him toward the door. "C'mon," he muttered. "Don't you have stock to check? There's the back corral to whitewash, too, if'n you run out of chores."

"Aw, cripes!" Dave replied, looking pained. "How come you get to be the foreman, anyhow?"

The two banged out the front door, leaving Slocum and Becky facing Tia Juanita, who simply said, "I have dishes waiting," and left the room.

Slocum stood there a moment in the suddenly vacant room, then asked, "Is it me?"

Becky laughed. It was awfully good to hear that after so many tears, and he laughed with her. She turned toward him, and through her laughter, said, "Would you like to see my bedroom, Slocum?"

Well, that was awful damn fine to hear, too!

"Lead on," he said.

She took him down the long back hall and opened the door to a large room furnished for a man, not a woman.

It had wood-paneled walls, plain and simple curtains, and next to no bric-a-brac. It was Jack Jamison's room, not Becky's.

She had brought one thing to it, though. Against the far wall in the corner sat an ornately carved, mahogany lowboy bureau. It was completely out of harmony with the rest of the spare, rough-hewn furnishings, but he remembered it from the last time he'd been to see Becky.

Of course, then it had been at the Bar S, which was now occupied by half-naked chicken-eaters.

He reminded himself to mention that to Becky later.

The bureau had a huge mirror attached to the back that rose up the wall, reflecting light from the opposite windows. On its top surface, there was a silver-backed hand mirror and a matching comb, a hair-keeper, and a buttonhook, along with containers for hairpins and hat pins and such, and a few framed photographs.

Yessir, that bureau and everything on it was all Becky.

He wondered why she hadn't changed the room after Jamison died, made it more frilly, more feminine. And then he wondered why, other than to bring the dresser over, she hadn't changed it in the first place, right after she'd married him.

He didn't have much time to mull it over, though, because just then Becky moved to stand in front of him. She put her hands on the flat of his chest.

"I want you to make love to me, Slocum," she said softly.

She didn't have to ask him twice. With his foot, he nudged the door closed behind them and heard it swing closed, then latch with a gentle *click*.

He touched her cheek. "You sure, honey? This quick?"

She nodded. "I'm sure as I've ever been about anything. I've been waiting for you for a very long time."

He kissed her, and as he did, he felt her hands rise up to his shoulders, then travel to hug his neck.

Like a wild mustang who'd just found water after too long in the desert, she threw herself into the kiss, drinking it deep, trying to drink him whole. Her tongue pushed gently against his, then roughly, and he returned the kiss for all he was worth.

He gave her all she wanted, and while he did, he pulled the pins from her upswept hair. Honey tresses toppled in soft waves, flowing down over her shoulders and back like a waterfall and smelling of soft lavender. Without breaking off the kiss, he scooped her up and in two strides he carried her to the bed.

He lay her down on the pale green bedspread, then broke away from her hungry mouth. Slit-eyed, swollen-lipped, she looked up at him.

She didn't say a word. Her face, her expression, said everything.

"All right, baby," he whispered. He quickly unbuttoned the bodice of her dress and pushed her camisole aside, freeing her breasts. They were still firm, high, and round, and were crowned with nipples of the palest, most delicate pink, which were now tightened and darkened with desire.

He brushed his lips over one erect nipple, and when Becky made a little growling sound deep in her throat, he took it into his mouth and twirled his tongue over the nub.

He felt her arching beneath him, as if she were trying to push more of her breast into his mouth, push her body more tightly against his, push her way into him. She was as heated and eager as if she'd been waiting all this time for him, just for him.

A little more roughly than he meant to, he pulled her dress down over her shoulders. He unfastened her belt with a quick turn of his wrist, and bared her to the waist. She let go of his neck just long enough to shrug her arms free of the dress.

But only one of her hands returned to the back of his

neck. The other went straight to his belt buckle, then his gunbelt.

She freed him, reached inside, and curled her fingers around him, and the intense heat and swelling he'd been feeling in his loins took on a whole new meaning. He felt himself growing even bigger in her grip when she began to rhythmically stroke him, softly squeeze him.

Suddenly, he removed his mouth from her bosom and in one motion, rolled and took her with him, so that she was on top.

He tugged at her skirts, and they finally went down over her slim hips, along with her petticoats and underwear. She wiggled out of them quickly, while he kicked his way free of his trousers and she tore at the buttons of his shirt.

Naked now, they kissed anew: frantically, urgently, and Slocum once again rolled on top of her. She opened her legs to him, cocking one over his back. She was already slippery wet, and he slid into her smoothly, slowly, as if they'd been made for each other.

She was close—very close—he knew it, and rather than try to catch up with her, he decided to let her finish. Besides, he thought as he began to drive into her, he was an old stud. Took him more than five minutes to get heated all the way up to a fever pitch. She seemed to have reached it in three.

He thrust deep into her, feeling her slippery inner walls grip him, hug him, cling to him as her breathing quickened and her eyes fluttered closed. She rose to meet his every driving thrust, and he tried to think about baseball, about shoeing horses, and about dismantling his rifle.

Halfway through his mental picture of the rifle, she suddenly froze, her back arched, and she sucked air in through her teeth. He felt her insides squeeze him tight— which just about did him in—and then she let out a low, deep, long moan before collapsing down on the bedspread.

Slocum, still inside her, dipped his head and let out a
long breath through his mouth. She had kindled a bonfire
in his loins. Oh, he'd been throwing metaphysical water
on it all right, but there wasn't enough imaginary water
in the world to put this fire out. He just had to give her
a chance to catch her breath before she could stoke it up
into a full-fledged conflagration.

"Slocum," she whispered, her eyes still closed, the
sooty lashes lying like moth wings on her pale cheeks.
Her breasts pressed against his chest. He could feel her
heart beating.

She really was astoundingly beautiful, he realized, and
not for the first time. How could he have forgotten it?

She murmured, "Did you . . . ?"

"Not yet," he murmured, kissing her forehead and her
temple, now damp with sweat. "That first one was a pres-
ent," he whispered huskily with an ornery grin. "Gonna
make you work for the next one, honey."

A soft smile curled her lips, and she opened her eyes
just a bit. She licked her lips. "Consider me on the payroll.
Go to it, boy."

And then she kissed him again.

It was an invitation of which he happily took advantage.

Tia Juanita, standing at the kitchen sink, smiled to herself
as she tended the dishes.

She paused for a moment, closed her eyes and said a
silent prayer of thanks to Our Lady of Guadalupe, then
crossed herself. Then she smiled. When Raul was alive,
he had said it was a miracle in itself that all her dresses
didn't have wear marks in the shape of a cross.

She sighed. Dear, sweet Raul. He had given her no
children—and she had given him none, as well—but he
had given her all of himself until the day he died.

She glanced out the window, and her soft smile turned

to a frown. There was Pete, walking across the yard from the big barn again. She leaned across the sink and out the window.

"Not now, Pete," she called. "Miss Becky, she is busy."

Pete stopped and propped one hand on his hip, his thumb through a belt loop. "Don't wanna see her. Want to talk to Slocum."

"He's busy, too," Tia Juanita shouted back. "You come back later."

Pete didn't give up, though. "Well, could you ask him where he got that horse? Me and Bill been havin' a discussion about it."

Tia Juanita sighed. Again, she called, "Come back later."

"Well, what are they doin' that they can't be—" Pete stopped midsentence, having had a revelation of sorts. Or at least, that's the way it looked by the expression on his face.

"Oh, cripes," she barely heard him mutter, and then he shouted, "Okay, Tia Juanita."

He turned and went back toward the barn, but not before Tia Juanita saw the smirk on his face.

Pete had been around when Slocum had come through Indian Springs the first time, three years ago. He and Dave should remember it well, seeing as how Slocum had saved both of their worthless lives. And too, they would do well to remember the flames that had sparked between Becky and Slocum.

She washed the last dish and wiped it dry, then pulled the plug in the sink. Jack Jamison had been very clever with the sink, rigging it to drain around the corner of the house and into the big flower bed. Tia Juanita was proud of her flowers, which were always brightly colored, no matter the season, and green-foliaged. Of course, they were also a beckoning home for black widow spiders.

She did not mind the spiders so much, she thought as

she began to dry the flatware. They had to live, too. But they also had to understand that when they spun their sticky, messy webs, lurking where people were going to dig or put their hands, they should expect to meet a fiery death.

She always burned them out with a small torch. It was the most efficient way. The spiders died with a satisfying *pop*, and it got the egg sacks, too.

Raul had taught her how to do it.

She glanced at the clock. Slocum and Becky had only been back there for about half an hour. Plenty of time for most men, Tia Juanita thought, but not for a tough old hombre like Slocum. That one, he could probably leave the gate and cross the finish line several times.

Especially when he was with a beautiful young filly like Becky.

Tia Juanita decided that she would not disturb them until it came time for supper. Becky and Slocum would have to eat, if for no other reason than to keep their strength up.

They were all going to be all right and safe, every last one of them. Except for Tate McMahon, of course.

Slocum would see to it.

And perhaps, this time, he would stay on for a while.

For the first time since the murder of Jack Jamison, Tia Juanita began to hum happily.

8

Five days after Tate McMahon sent out the telegrams, Drug Cassidy rode into Indian Springs.

Cassidy was a middle-sized man both in height and girth, plain-faced, middle-aged, and all around average. This had always stood him in good stead.

When he had a drink in the saloon or doffed his hat to a lady on the street, nobody ever suspected that such an ordinary fellow could be the famous Drugman Cassidy, fresh in from Colorado Springs, and casting an eye about for the man—or men—he'd been hired to kill. Or, more often these days, the range war he'd been hired to break up.

It was a living, he told himself. And after all, he wasn't getting any younger. There were other problems, too.

McMahon hadn't been very specific in his wire. The only part with any substance to it had been the part that offered five hundred dollars. A number like that carried a lot of weight with Drugman Cassidy. Especially since it didn't sound like much work. He just had to pry one pesky fellow out of the way.

Of course, it seemed a little queer that McMahon couldn't just hire somebody local to get rid of this pest.

Either that, or pay him off. McMahon was the big fish in this part of the pond: At least, he was by the look of the signs on the storefronts that Cassidy passed.

Enough money could work miracles.

He wandered slowly down the street, taking his time, picking his teeth, taking it all in, until he had ambled north all the way up Main Street, and then back south to the other end. What few side streets there were just seemed to have private houses on them, a few with feeble and struggling gardens, but most with nothing but unkept cactus and weeds.

There weren't many folks on the street, but they all had a vaguely furtive look. Sort of haunted, but without their knowing it.

He'd been in enough towns—and seen enough people—like this to recognize it, even if the citizens didn't. It was a town on the verge of being enclosed in a stranglehold, and he had a pretty good idea he was working for the man who was planning on doing the strangling.

Well, he'd see.

He turned around and walked slowly back up to what he figured was Tate McMahon's office, which was situated on the east side of the street. MCMAHON ENTERPRISES, read the sign.

He walked in.

The first thing he saw was Teddy LeGrande, and Cassidy nearly drew his weapon. What stopped him was the fact that there was a second man in the room, sitting behind the desk with his boots up on it, who said, "Mr. Cassidy, I presume?"

Cassidy flicked the tie-down off his gun, but didn't draw it. Even though Teddy LeGrande surely deserved killing after that trick he'd pulled back in Jackson Hole, Wyoming, Cassidy put a lid on it. He figured to reconnoiter the situation first.

Teddy LeGrande had roughly the same reaction as Cassidy. He was a big man, about six-feet-two, and lean and wiry as a whip. He was also stupid, something Cassidy figured anybody with a brain could tell just by looking at that big, dumb farmer face and those weak, dull, little eyes.

Pig eyes, he'd once heard his daddy call eyes like that. They looked more like two piss holes in the snow to Drug Cassidy.

Aside from those two beady black eyes, the rest of Teddy LeGrande was practically all white, or off-white. He had real pale skin, like a banker or a woman, and pale yellow hair. It was his affectation to dress all in white, too, which he thought made him look more fearsome.

The idiot.

Tate McMahon seemed to have fallen for all LeGrande's window dressing, though, because he looked right disappointed when Cassidy, who knew he appeared as common as a mud fence, said, "Yeah, I'm Cassidy. You McMahon?"

Well, let him be disappointed. Let him think what he wanted.

After a split second, though, McMahon recovered. He took his damned boots off his desk and stood up, extending his hand. Cassidy took it, but only because his daddy had taught him to be polite to people who were going to pay him five hundred dollars.

"Pleased to meet you, Cassidy!" crowed McMahon.

Cassidy just grunted.

McMahon sat down again, looking pleased with himself.

"This feller you want," said LeGrande. "Why's he so big he needs two guns to take him out?"

It was the exact question Cassidy would have asked, had LeGrande not beaten him to it. Damn him, anyhow. And he'd taken to wearing a white leather jacket with long fringe on the sleeves, Cassidy realized.

Of all the goddamned stupid things! Didn't it get in the way of his gun hand? Mayhap he just hadn't noticed it yet.

Be a real shame if he was to find it out in the middle of a gunfight, Cassidy thought, and almost smiled.

"The gentleman in question—and I use the term with quite a bit of charity—has been through here before," Mc-Mahon replied. "Cleaned out this town about three years back, before I got here. 'Course, that only opened it up for me."

The boots went back up on the desk. This fellow sure thought highly of himself, didn't he? There weren't that many men who'd relax in the company of Teddy Le-Grande.

Or, if they'd managed to figure out who he was, Drug-man Cassidy.

But this fellow was cocky. Cassidy supposed that owning a town could make you that way. But owning a town couldn't make you slick, the way Tate McMahon was. No, you had to have been born that way. McMahon was lean and of medium height, gray at the temples, with a short, neat haircut—he practically still had talc on his neck—and pale, pale blue eyes, like ice.

He was a nice-looking man. He could have walked right out of a hair tonic ad, in fact. But there was still just a hint of larceny around his eyes and a touch of deceit around his mouth. And Cassidy figured the man to be in a real good mood right now, what with both his hired guns turning up on the same day.

Those were the kind of eyes and mouth that could smile up a storm while the brain behind them was plotting to kill you.

All this, Drug Cassidy thought in the fraction of a second it took McMahon to raise his boots again and thump them down on the desk top.

He'd always been good at sizing men up.

However, he pushed all that aside, and concentrated on the job at hand. After all, five hundred bucks was five hundred bucks.

Cassidy said, "Get to the point, McMahon. Who's this saddle bum you want shed of?"

McMahon laced his fingers behind his neck and grinned. "You boys ever hear of some sonofabitch, calls himself Slocum?"

During those five days, Slocum had been busy, too. He'd ridden out to the distant corner of the ranch where Jack Jamison had been bushwhacked and murdered, and gone over all the ground for a good hundred and fifty yards in every direction.

He turned up nothing but a couple of rifle shell casings and a piece of treated deer hide caught on a thorn. He stuck these in his pocket.

The casings were unusual, because they were engraved with a curious design, the origin of which Slocum didn't recognize. They were a sort of panther's head, crudely tapped in and not quite matching from one casing to the other. Somebody was marking his casings after he bought the ammunition, because it sure wasn't a factory stamp.

He hadn't expected to find anything more. He hadn't even expected to find those shell casings. Jack Jamison had been shot from a distance, Becky had told him.

And, from what he had seen, by a man who had been lurking up in the rocks.

He'd been a sniper, Slocum decided, and a good one at that. He'd picked his spot well, and probably lain there quietly for Jack Jamison to ride into range. Slocum had been an assassin himself back during the war, trained to shoot from the boughs of faraway trees at solitary victims.

He hadn't had much taste for it, although he was good. He was the best.

Of course, rifles back then didn't have special scopes

the way they did nowadays, but Slocum was a good enough shot himself to see that whoever had killed Jack Jamison had to be a contract man, brought in just for that job.

It wasn't the sort of thing an ordinary man, even an ordinary hired killer, could pull off. The sniper was probably long gone by now. He'd probably left the second he got paid.

All he'd left behind was that little chunk of leather and two empty casings.

And the body of Jack Jamison.

Becky had said that she hadn't loved Jack. At least, not in the flowery poetry and pounding hearts kind of way.

She said he'd been good to her, which Slocum figured meant that at least he didn't beat her or make her sleep in the barn.

No, Becky said she hadn't loved him, but Slocum didn't think that was entirely true. He didn't see a gal like Becky marrying for something so common as her economic betterment.

Besides, she'd inherited the Bar S from her daddy. It was why she'd come to the Territory in the first place. She hadn't needed the money and she hadn't needed a white knight. At least, once Slocum had got rid of Roy Wheeler for her. And for the whole town of Indian Springs, as a matter of fact.

No, she'd had to have some sort of love for Jack Jamison in order to marry him.

Slocum couldn't decide how he felt about that. Why, sometimes he got so pure jealous of that dead man that if Jamison had still been walking, Slocum could have killed him all over again! Or at least punched him in the jaw.

Sometimes he went mushy as a hound dog pup with gratitude, thinking about how his Becky had been taken care of after he left. Those episodes didn't last too long, though.

And it wasn't as if he wouldn't leave again, once he got this thing figured out.

He'd talked with Becky at length, and he'd talked with the hands, who he learned had just come back from moving the herd down to the south, to the winter grazing lands. Then, with Becky, he'd ridden down to the old Bar S, read that chicken-eating cowhand the riot act, and quite literally kicked him out of the house.

The cowhand had been in his long johns at the time. Slocum had enjoyed that part.

She had showed him her goats, all fifty-plus of them. He'd shaken hands with all the help, from the men who tended the flock to the men who milked the goats and made the cheese in the long, adobe building out back of the house. They were all new since his time, and he hadn't recognized a one of them.

Becky took him down to see the aging room they had cut out of the hard desert floor. And there, fifteen feet below the ground, amid hundreds of small, fragrant cheeses wrapped in gauze and hanging from the ceiling beams, he'd made love to her.

He'd been doing quite a bit of that, lately.

Not that he minded.

Not at all, ma'am, glad to oblige.

But today he was going to take a ride into town and have a look around. He wanted to figure out just what Tate McMahon had up his sleeve for the next time. He knew it wouldn't be a forced marriage again. At least, not right away. McMahon would have to get rid of him first.

And to get rid of Slocum, McMahon would have to kill him.

Slocum figured that there should be a few folks in town who remembered him fondly—or at least who wouldn't shoot him on sight, he thought with a quick grin. He wanted to know about anybody who was new in town.

Any further information he could dig up on Tate Mc-
Mahon would be a bonus, too.

He saddled up Concho, pausing to admire the gelding
once more. Damn, he was a nice piece of horseflesh, especially when you hadn't really seen him for a spell. Slocum hadn't seen him that much, aside for occasional rides
here and there. Most of his time had been taken up with
Becky: with touching her, with making love to her, with
just plain looking at her.

"Well, I reckon that's important, too," he said with a
grin, and mounted up. "You understand, don't you, old
son?"

Then again, the Appy was a gelding. He probably
didn't understand.

He probably didn't give a damn, either.

"Hey, Slocum!" shouted a voice.

There was Pete, leading his horse, tacked up and ready
to go, out of the barn.

"I'm comin' with you," Pete announced, and swung up
into the saddle.

"No, you're not," Slocum said. They'd been through
this before. Pete was a hell of a man, even though he'd
acted a little on the addled side that first day Slocum had
ridden into the S Bar J. He was honest, for one thing, and
he was a good hand with stock. And a gun.

Slocum didn't want him along, though.

"I'm comin'," Pete said again, and reined his mount
over to where Slocum sat Concho. "Miss Becky says go,
and I'm goin'." He whoaed his bay up, shoulder to shoulder with Concho.

Slocum sighed. He hated to do it, but he would. He
said, "You ain't gonna take no for an answer, are you?"

Stubbornly, Pete shook his head.

"Sorry, ol' buddy," said Slocum, and suddenly swung
an arm over the space between them to punch Pete in the
side of the jaw.

Like he figured, Pete went right off his horse. There were some things you just couldn't help but remember about a fellow, and a glass jaw was one of them.

"Dammit, Slocum!" The screen door banged and he heard Becky yelling at him.

He didn't look back, although he knew she was running toward him with those pretty hands balled into fists and her mouth set into a line.

Instead, he tipped his hat to the unconscious Pete, whose horse was nuzzling him as he lay on the ground, and rode out, heading for the crossroad that would take him to town.

9

"You just let him ride out by himself!" Becky Jamison said angrily, and for the third or fourth time. "All alone!"

Pete, holding a damp cloth to his jaw, looked up guiltily but said nothing.

"Oh, Pete!" she said in nearly a shout. "I could just throttle you!"

He hung his head, cringing slightly. "Yes'm. Reckon you could. I mean, I tried, but—"

Waving a hand, she sighed heavily and dropped into the chair next to him, at the table. "I'm sorry, Pete," she said wearily. "I mean, I'm sorry Slocum hit you. Are you hurt bad? Is it broken?"

"No, ma'am," came the muttered reply. "I mean, I think I'll be okay." He stuck a finger in his mouth as if wiggling a few teeth, then added, "Least he didn't knock out any of my chewin' teeth."

Becky wasn't paying too much attention, though. She could just imagine Slocum, nonchalantly belting poor Pete in the mouth and knocking him off his horse. When she had come out the door Pete was already down. And out like a lamp.

Men, men, men. Knee deep in male hormones, that's

what they were, and most of them were Slocum's. Honestly! He and Pete were both idiots, when you got right down to it.

All right, they were all three idiots, counting her. She supposed she'd contributed her fair share to all the leg-lifting going on lately, if only as a cheerleader.

And the truth was that she really didn't know why she'd fought Tate McMahon so bitterly and for so long and so hard.

It wasn't that she was courageous.

It wasn't as if she couldn't go back east.

It wasn't even that she was driven to stay here, on this land, because of some sort of ancestral connection to it.

Perhaps it was because, she thought, she was just too damned stubborn to do anything else. Especially when somebody she found distasteful in the first place was pressuring her to leave.

Distasteful? She snorted softly. My, she was suddenly being very ladylike about Tate McMahon, wasn't she?

A murdering, thieving, double-dealing, blackguard, yellow-bellied bastard of a sonofabitch would have been more on the order of it.

"Miss Becky?" came Tia Juanita's voice.

Becky looked up.

"You were miles away from here," Tia Juanita said quietly.

Becky nodded. "I suppose I was. Pete, do you feel up to riding now?"

Pete answered with an unsure, "Yup," and started to rise, but Tia Juanita pushed him back in his chair with a firm hand.

"No one rides anywhere, Becky Sawyer Jamison," she said with that expression that meant *don't mess with me if you know what's good for you!* Becky was all too familiar with it.

Becky closed her eyes for a moment, if for no other

reason than self-defense. "For heaven's sake, why?"

The dish towel, ever-present in Tia Juanita's hands or looped over her apron, twisted loosely between her fingers. "Slocum needs no one to baby-sit with him," she said firmly. "He is a grown man. He is very good at what he does. If he says he will ride into town alone, he will go alone."

The housekeeper turned her gaze to Pete. "There is a reason for this, Pete. I think he thought that hitting you was better than what might happen if you were to go along with him. I think Slocum is usually right about these things, and I think you should count yourself lucky."

Pete looked up, still holding the damp cloth to his jaw, and blinked. "If this is lucky, I'd sure hate to set an eye on unlucky."

Tia Juanita set her mouth and furrowed her brows. "Unlucky is what would have happened three years ago, if Slocum had not come. Do you forget how he saved you and Dave? How he pulled your worthless carcasses from the river?"

Pete sat back with a *thump* and muttered, "After that no-count dub Wheeler had his boys tie us up and toss us in to drown."

Leaning back in her chair, Becky drummed her fingertips on the table, barely listening.

"I suppose you're right, Tia Juanita," she said at last, and reluctantly. "It's just . . . Pete, do you feel well enough to leave us?"

"Huh?" he said, then scrambled to his feet and handed his jaw cloth to Tia Juanita. "Sure. Yes, ma'am, I'll give you some privacy. Gotta see to my horse, anyways."

Becky waited until the screen door slammed behind him before she spoke again.

"It's just that I can't bear the thought of something happening to Slocum," she admitted, and felt hot tears pushing at the backs of her eyes. She managed to hold them in check, though.

Tia Juanita sat down in the chair that Pete had vacated, and scooted it closer. Leaning forward, she put her arm around Becky's shoulders.

"I know, my peach," she soothed. "I know how you worry. But you must remember that he is his own man. He has very much . . . how do you say? In Spanish, we call it *machismo*. He must do what he wishes, and when. And how. You must not interfere. In anything he decides to do."

Becky stared at her a long time before she said, "You're telling me something else, too, aren't you, Tia Juanita?"

"Yes, angel," the housekeeper said, and tucked an errant strand of hair back behind Becky's ear. "And I think you know what it is. Be prepared."

Becky lowered her gaze. She could try to be prepared for his going, but that didn't mean she'd have to like it.

But a man had to do what a man had to do.

Dammit.

Drug Cassidy sat quietly at the bar's back table, nursing a beer and staring out over the small crowd. Although mostly, he was looking at the show going on up front.

He snorted softly in disgust.

Teddy LeGrande ought to go on the stage—preferably, one far away from here. China, for instance.

At the moment, he was holding court along the bar rail, white fringe swinging as he gestured and talked. He had an audience of exactly three men, cowhand types, who probably worked for Tate McMahon.

He was a good-enough-looking fellow, Cassidy supposed, until he opened his mouth. He shuddered to think what a blithering asshole LeGrande would be in front of a crowd of fifty. Hell, they could just pass out the shovels at the door.

Of course, in a crowd of fifty, there'd more likely be

somebody who'd just shoot him to shut him up.

Cassidy liked that idea.

"Once, when I was up on the Platte . . ." LeGrande was saying.

Cassidy tried not to hear him. LeGrande was messing up his life yet again, this time by making a whole lot of useless noise when there was thinking to be done.

He comforted himself that LeGrande hadn't done something totally idiotic, like point him out and introduce him as the famous Drugman Cassidy. Of course not. That would have taken attention away from LeGrande, Cassidy thought. He smirked in spite of himself.

Well, he'd be thankful for small favors, like his daddy had taught him.

It had been a long time since he'd run into John Slocum. Oh, he hadn't let on to LeGrande or McMahon. LeGrande had said as how he thought as how he'd heard the name Slocum, heard he had a reputation, so he was roughly equal to McMahon on that count.

And Cassidy? He'd just shrugged.

McMahon had looked at him as if he were an idiot, as if he couldn't imagine why he'd sent for him in the first place.

"Hell, every son of a buck over the age of five's heard of him!" McMahon had sneered with the vast superiority of one who had just come into this knowledge himself.

"Where do you live, anyhow?" McMahon had asked incredulously. "Under a goddamn barrel? Keep up to date, man!"

It was just as well.

The less anybody knew, the better.

Cassidy thought it fairly odd when McMahon confided to them that Slocum had steered clear of town these past five days.

McMahon had been pretty damned cocky about it, too, as if he figured Slocum's absence so far meant that Slocum was afraid of him.

But Cassidy knew Slocum's ways better than that. For one thing, he knew that Slocum must have a woman out at that ranch. Cassidy figured it was the only thing that could distract him. Of course, McMahon hadn't mentioned a woman, not yet, but there was certain to be one mixed up in this deal someplace.

As a matter of fact, McMahon hadn't mentioned much of anything about why he wanted Slocum killed, just some sort of vague reason. "He's in my way," or some crud like that.

Did Tate McMahon think his fancy hired guns were fools?

Cassidy supposed that if you took LeGrande into consideration, McMahon was half right.

He caught the bartender's eye and signaled for another beer. It wasn't the best and it was warm besides, but the stuff settled the trail dust in your throat.

So. What to do about Slocum? After all, there was five hundred involved.

Just as the bartender slid another warm beer sloshing on Cassidy's table, the batwing doors of the McMahon Palace swung inward, pushed by a very large and powerful frame.

Slocum.

LeGrande, the idiot, didn't recognize him. He just gave Slocum a dismissive glance, then kept on talking. Cassidy saw Slocum lift his brows almost imperceptibly as he passed, making silent comment on the show—and the show-boater—at the bar.

Two steps later, Slocum locked eyes with Cassidy. His expression started to alter, but Cassidy gave his head a tiny shake—no, not now, dammit—and Slocum abruptly turned and sidled up to the bar rail, about halfway between himself and Teddy LeGrande.

"Beer," he heard Slocum say softly as he propped his elbow, then dropped a coin on the bar's polished surface.

It spun and spun, sparkling in the light from the front windows, then jangled to a rest.

Five hundred dollars, Cassidy thought with a sad shake of his head. *Christ on a crutch.*

10

"Slocum? I've heard of him, all right!"

The speaker, not much more than a kid, had just entered the bar, and his ears had perked up right away at the overheard mention of Slocum's name. Teddy LeGrande was the man he was addressing.

Slocum's ears had perked up, too, but he hadn't been so foolish as to show it. Suddenly, Drug Cassidy's presence was forgotten. All Slocum could hear was the kid.

"Sure, I heard of him! Fastest gun in the Territory," the boy went on energetically. "Some say fastest this side of the Big Muddy!"

The kid was maybe nineteen years old, dark-haired and good-looking, but with that overeager demeanor that Slocum had come to loathe.

The boy wasn't wearing a gun—didn't look like he'd ever strapped one on—but Slocum pegged his type right away. His worn cuffs bore ink stains and he probably worked as a minor clerk at some office or other. But he stamped a mental label on him and filed him away under the general heading of "Fool."

The man who had dropped his name was the same son-ofabitch who'd been orating, up toward the front of the bar. Slocum hadn't said a word—'fact, the fellow was hardly aware of his existence—but Slocum had learned a whole lot about him inside of just three minutes.

The white-fringed dandy was called Teddy LeGrande, although that meant nothing to Slocum. LeGrande was out of Santa Fe, and he'd come here to do some kind of job, although he was elusive—in a winking way—about just what that might be.

Slocum knew, though. In these parts, Tate McMahon was the only man with the wherewithal to put a hired gun on his payroll, even a rigged-up, rigged-out gun like this one.

And it appeared that LeGrande wasn't the only gun McMahon had hired. Drug Cassidy's appearance in town was just too goddamn coincidental. Of course, that bastard Cassidy had the good sense to sit back and not call attention to himself, unlike the fringed dandy at the bar.

So did Slocum, for that matter.

Teddy LeGrande's eyes narrowed, and for the first time Slocum saw that there was a killer lurking beneath the Wild West Show veneer.

LeGrande stared at the kid and said, "You seen him?"

The boy, too, reacted to the sudden change in Le-Grande's demeanor.

He gulped and said, "N-no, sir. I was only sayin' that I heard of him. He's supposed to be faster'n greased lightning! Why, he took out Big Ricky Trumble up in Wyoming! He shot it out with the Piper brothers down in Nogales and killed 'em both. He—"

"Would you know him if you was to see him?" Le-Grande cut in, without altering his expression.

"I . . . I guess not," the boy admitted. "I never see'd him afore. But I heard—"

"Don't believe everything you hear, kid," LeGrande said, his amiable smile returning. "Now, beat it."

The boy turned, but not before LeGrande theatrically

raised a foot and booted him in the leg. The kid stumbled and fell.

Both members of LeGrande's audience found this hilarious, as did LeGrande.

The boy's features knotted and his hands flexed into fists, but he picked himself up and backed away, out of range.

"Your big hero, Slocum, can't hold a candle to Teddy LeGrande, boy," LeGrande said through his laughter.

Don't ask him, kid, Slocum thought with an audible groan.

But the boy did anyhow. Rubbing his thigh, he asked angrily, "So, who's Teddy LeGrande?"

Slocum sighed. From the corner of his eye, he saw Drug Cassidy, at the rear table, stiffen almost imperceptibly. His right hand stayed on the table top, though.

Well, that was good, Slocum supposed. Two times now, Cassidy had proved that he didn't want any trouble. Public trouble, anyway.

He flicked his gaze back up front.

"Hold this," LeGrande was saying. He tossed the boy a silver dollar.

Fumbling, the lad caught the cartwheel and clutched it to his chest dumbly. He'd probably just stopped in here for a quick beer on the way home. He was dressed like a petty clerk. Neat and clean, but a little worn around the edges, and quite possibly underpaid.

And he probably spent too much money on dime novels for his own good.

"Hold it up, boy, 'less you want to take a slug where you're holdin' it now," said LeGrande.

Once again, the boys at the bar thought this was pretty damned funny.

The kid didn't, though. Trembling, he held the coin up with his left hand, barely gripping it by the edge.

"Back up," LeGrande demanded.

The kid backed all the way to the wall and hit it with

a *thump* as LeGrande drew his gun. There was more laughter from the yokels at the bar.

And Slocum was thinking that this was the kind of kid, who, if he lived through this episode, was liable to come after LeGrande with a gun. He looked fool enough.

With no further thought, Slocum moved to intervene. But before he could take a single step, Teddy LeGrande fired.

The silver cartwheel flew into the air as the kid yelped and stuck his fingers in his mouth. LeGrande now joined in the laughter.

"Pick that up and take 'er with you," he said. He twirled his gun on his index finger, then jammed it back into its holster. Quite grandly, he added, "A keepsake of the time you met Teddy LeGrande, for real and in person."

Pulling his fingers from his mouth only to stick them beneath his armpit, the kid nearly cried, "You busted my finger!"

LeGrande cocked a brow. "Be glad that was all," he said, then turned his back on the boy. "Another one," he said, and slid his empty mug spinning toward the barkeep.

The boy, powerless and near tears, bent and scooped up the silver dollar with his good hand, pausing to peer at it. Slocum saw the bullet hole drilled through it before the kid shoved it in his pocket.

Not too proud to take that souvenir, though, are you, junior?

Slocum shook his head tiredly. It was getting so that his life had turned into a series of repeating loops. The details changed, but the basics remained the same.

And he thought, for not the first time, that he was getting too old for this horseshit.

The boy stood there a moment, behind the back of Teddy LeGrande, as if considering his options and finally seeing none at all. Angrily, he banged out the batwing doors, presumably on his way to visit the doctor.

Slocum noted that it was his left hand that had been

injured. Too bad. A busted up right one would save them all a whole lot of grief later on.

Of course, he could be wrong.

He hoped he would be.

He flicked a glance back toward Drug Cassidy, who remained in the same place, sipping the last of his beer and apparently unfazed. Amazing how he just faded into the background like that. It must be a goddamned gift or something.

Slocum knew that even though Drug Cassidy's attention seemed to be focused on his beer mug, he was aware of everything and everybody in the place, as well as what was going on out on the street. Hell, probably in the shop-front next door, too!

Sneaky old peckerwood.

And then Drug Cassidy stood up, stretched, and slowly ambled from the bar as anonymously as Slocum imagined he'd come in.

It's about time I took care of this, Slocum thought, and reluctantly gulped down the last of his beer.

He thumbed the strap from his hammer before he walked past Teddy LeGrande, but there was no need. LeGrande was so swept up in his own story—this one was a real horse-choker about shooting Boss Tucker in a duel on the streets of Dodge City—that he didn't even notice Slocum's passing.

Slocum stepped outside, glanced right, then left. No sign of Cassidy.

It figured.

Cassidy had planted himself just inside the mouth of an alley about halfway between the McMahon Palace and the McMahon Livery, and waited, his hand resting impatiently on the butt of his gun.

When he heard the echoing boot steps approaching on the boardwalk, he stiffened and stood erect, poised to move.

"Shut up!" he hissed at the precise moment that he stepped forward, grabbed Slocum, and hauled him into the alley.

Slocum didn't fight him, but wrestled free almost instantly and turned on him, gun drawn.

Cassidy raised his hands and took a step backward, farther into the alley. "I give up, you sonofabitch," he said. "Don't shoot."

Slocum stood there for a second, expressionless, before he jammed his gun back down in its holster and asked, "What the hell's goin' on, Drug?"

Cassidy sniffed. "Glad to see you, too," he said dryly. "You know, there's five hundred, cash, on your lousy head. You ought'a thank me for not pluggin' you on sight and draggin' your carcass back down the street for the cash."

"McMahon hire you?" Slocum asked, taking another step deeper into the alley, into the shadows.

Standing there in the cramped space between barrels and crates, across from Slocum, Cassidy realized again what a powerful man he was.

He must have half-expected to be tackled somewhere along the way, or Cassidy never would have been able to drag him as far as he had. Which hadn't been all that far.

"Yeah, he did," Cassidy answered. "And that big theatrical lamebrain in all the fringe, too." He hiked a thumb up the street, toward the saloon. "Reckon that means there's actually a thousand on you, Slocum, if McMahon offered him the same as me. Y'know, I could just shoot you right here and claim my reward and Teddy LeGrande's, too. I could really use me a thousand bucks."

Slocum actually grinned. "Sure, Drug. Try it."

A smile crept across Cassidy's face, too. "Think I'd druther go over to the other side. I take a real strong exception to any man who'd have the nerve to hire both Teddy LeGrande and me to do the same job. Hell, that idiot did me out of a four-hundred-dollar reward up in Jackson Hole!"

Slocum, situating himself so that he was covered by the late-afternoon shadows—and so that he still had a good view of the street—pulled out his fixings bag and began to roll a smoke.

As he bent the paper into a V, he asked, "How'd he pull that off?"

"Oh, he just snuck up and bushwhacked me while I was sleepin'," Cassidy replied. "Hogtied me, then let my prisoner go, so's he could shoot him ten feet later. Left me trussed up like a Christmas goose, and turned my prisoner's body in."

Cassidy shook his head. "And here I was, tryin' to be all Christianlike, not shootin' the sonofabitch myself when the paper on him said dead or alive."

Slocum stuck his quirlie into his mouth, flicked a sulphurtip into flame, lit it, and smiled. Around it, he said, "That'll teach you to sleep." He shook out the match.

"Yup," said Cassidy, bitterly. "Thing is, Teddy's so dumb he figures it's some sort'a joke. He don't figure I should be all that het up about it, the big, pig-eyed jerk."

"Did McMahon bring anybody else in?" Slocum asked, staring not at Cassidy, but out toward the sunlit street.

"Not that I know of. Guess he figures two against one is good enough odds for anybody."

Slocum snorted.

"There's a woman mixed up in it, too, ain't there?" Cassidy asked.

Slocum cocked a brow. "He didn't tell you much, did he?"

"Nope."

Slocum sighed. "Yeah, there's a woman."

"Always is," Cassidy said, happy to have been right.

Slocum looked a tad irritated, but went on, "Lady named Becky Jamison out west of town. She's the final holdout. McMahon's spent the last year and a half buying everybody else out, though I sure can't figure out why.

Hell, the land's so rugged and rocky up here that it takes two acres to feed one steer! Anyhow, when he couldn't high-pressure her husband, he shot him. Had him shot, I mean. That was about six months ago."

"I'm pure sorry to hear that, Slocum," Cassidy interjected.

"Yeah," said Slocum, without expression. "You wouldn't know of a distance marksman who was travelin' out here on a job of work back then, would you? Marks his cartridges with a big cat scratched into the brass?"

"Nope," said Cassidy after some thought. "And don't go lookin' at me. I can't draw a cougar or a jaguar worth beans, and if you're addlepated enough to think it was me that done it, hell, I ain't any good past a hundred feet or so."

Actually, it was more like forty feet these last few years, but he didn't say so. And Slocum was kind enough not to say so, either.

Cassidy knew there was a reason he liked the big man.

Cassidy also knew his eyesight was failing these last few years. Lately, it was faster all the time. He'd been to see a couple of doctors, and after a lot of looking and humphing and so on, they'd both told him the same thing. Retinal something-or-other. He had a blind spot right dead center of his left eye, which he had to close to fire, and his right eye was all messed up. Objects seemed to just run downhill and trail away to nothing, even when he knew damn well they were there and solid.

The upshot of which was that he'd be blind inside five years.

But he figured he could see almost good enough right now. Good enough to get along, that was. He'd learned to compensate for it. And he didn't like to think about it. He'd rather think about the business at hand.

"Tell me the rest," Cassidy said.

"I'll tell you as much as I know," Slocum replied, "but it ain't much."

11

"Where you been?" Teddy LeGrande asked, carefully straightening his fringe. "You disappeared."

"Around," replied Cassidy. He had left Slocum a good half-hour ago, and had just wandered back up to the saloon. "What business is it of yours, anyhow? I mean, now that you've decided to come down off your damn perch and speak to me."

The remark had no effect on LeGrande. Cassidy hadn't expected it to.

"There was fellas in here before," Teddy LeGrande said, as if that explained everything. Actually, it did. The McMahon Palace was now vacant of any customers other than themselves. They stood shoulder to shoulder at the rail, making eye contact only in the mirrored bar-back. He said, "You still didn't tell me where you was."

"If it's any of your nevermind, which it ain't," Cassidy said, "I been askin' around town nice and easy-like. Seems Slocum ain't been in town. Or so says the general populace."

Teddy LeGrande looked confused, and Cassidy added, "That's what the people tell me, leastwise."

"Oh," said LeGrande, and took another sip of his beer.

"So, how you wanna do this thing? Just ride out there and shoot him, or what?"

Cassidy's mouth muscles clenched up for a moment. He really ought to just say, *Sure thing, Teddy*, and let LeGrande ride out there bold as brass. And let Slocum shoot him square in the butt. But he'd made a promise to Slocum.

"That there would be a real bad idea, Teddy," he said.

LeGrande smiled. "Hey, you're callin' me by my name. I knew you wasn't really mad about that bounty deal. Fellers like you an' me got to stick together, right?"

Cassidy didn't answer. He took a drink, then stared at his beer. This was going to be harder than he'd thought. If it had been anybody else other than Slocum who had asked him to hold off . . .

"Well, you got any other suggestions, Drug?" Le-Grande went on. "You don't mind if I call you Drug, do you?"

"Sure," said Cassidy, meaning, *yes, I sure do mind it, you rigged-out, fancified asshole.*

"Good, Drug," LeGrande said, impervious. "Things'll be easier if we're friends. You know? So what you figure? We wait for Slocum to come into town, then?"

Cassidy could bear the conversation no longer. He said, "Let me get back to you on that, Teddy. Want to think on it for a spell."

LeGrande seemed relieved. Whether it was that he wouldn't have to do anything complicated—for instance figuring out a plot of his own—or that he was just happy to have help, having learned a little more about Slocum, was beside the point.

But as usual, LeGrande didn't know when to quit.

"That's good, Drug, real good," he said. "To tell you the truth, I been a tad-mite worried about this deal."

When Cassidy said nothing, LeGrande went on, "I mean, what with hearin' so many stories 'bout this Slocum character." He glanced to both sides, then lowered his voice. "You think he's really as fast as they say?"

LeGrande was looking anxious, now, and for a moment, Cassidy wondered if he should just scare him off. By the looks of things, it would be fairly easy to do.

But Cassidy had promised Slocum. Plus, he figured, if LeGrande tucked his tail and headed home, McMahon might not trust him to take care of things on his own. McMahon might just bring in somebody else.

Even a fancy-assed, pretty-boy louse like Teddy Le-Grande was a sight better than an undrawn card. Like his daddy had said, you'd best stick with the devil you know and the cards you're dealt.

Although he wasn't too sure about his daddy's wisdom on the card thing.

He knew LeGrande could be tough when he was in a spot. Experience had taught Cassidy to read what was behind those eyes of LeGrande's. But being tough when push came to shove still didn't cancel out that streak of cowardice he'd just uncovered.

Before, he'd figured LeGrande for just a plain idiot. Now he figured him for a chicken, too. And he was beginning to wonder just how LeGrande had come by that reputation of his.

Cassidy said, "Yeah, Teddy, I think he probably is pretty damn fast with a gun."

"But he ain't come into town yet," LeGrande said, more to himself than to Cassidy. He stared directly at his own reflection in the bar mirror, not noticing that Cassidy was staring at him, too.

And suddenly Cassidy saw something else flickering there, something that had lurked beneath the facade of being either frightened or foolish or just plain stupid: It was something cruel and primitive.

A shiver went through him, unbidden.

And his first thought was that he and Slocum could very well be in a world of trouble.

Slocum finished putting Concho up in the barn before he announced himself at the house. He wanted a word with Pete and Dave and the boys, anyhow. That finished, he stepped up on the porch, stomped the dust off his boots, then opened the door.

"Anybody home?" he called when he found the parlor and kitchen empty. Even Tia Juanita had disappeared—a disappointment, because he'd had his mouth all set for a mess of her good cooking.

Hell, the stove wasn't even hot!

He called out again when nobody answered his first shout, but the house remained silent.

"What the hell?" he muttered beneath his breath. Pete hadn't mentioned the women were gone. Nobody had mentioned it.

And then he got to thinking that maybe Teddy Le-Grande had headed out while he was in that alley, talking with Cassidy, and that LeGrande had snuck in and taken them someplace. Probably killed them.

Those idiot hands! They hadn't heard or seen a thing, goddamnit!

He was halfway out the front door, ready to punch Pete's lights out, when both Becky and Tia Juanita rounded the corner of the porch. They were chattering happily, and their arms were full of flowers.

Slocum was so tense that "Dammit, Becky!" was the first thing that came out of his mouth.

Both women stopped, and Becky blinked. "I was going to say welcome back," she said. "But if you're going to be that nasty for no apparent reason, you can just go back to town."

"Sorry," he said, and relaxed. "I thought somethin' had happened to you."

"Well, it hasn't," Becky said curtly, stepping forward. Tia Juanita followed her. "We were just picking the last of the flowers before the cold snap, that's all," she continued. "Tia Juanita says there's one coming tonight."

"Yes," said Tia Juanita. "I feel it in my old bones."

Becky held one forward—he didn't know what kind, not being much for flowers—and passed it beneath Slocum's nose. "Smells pretty, doesn't it?"

"Yeah," he said with a steady grin. "Smells like you."

Tia Juanita took Becky's flowers. Her arms brimming, she walked past them both, into the house. Slocum waited until the door had closed behind her to pull Becky into his arms.

In the west, the sun was slowly nearing the horizon. Pink and soft purple traces were already starting to streak the sky.

"I don't know about that cold snap," he said. "Seems pretty warm around here to me."

Playfully, she pushed at his chest. "Tia Juanita's got the last word about the weather on this ranch. Besides, you know how the high desert can be. Hot in the daytime—"

"Freezing at night," he finished for her. "Except in our bed."

They kissed long and sweet, and when they were finally finished, Becky whispered, "I hate to break the mood, honey, but did you find anything out today? You nearly frightened me to death, riding off by yourself like that."

He shook his head. "Women. You don't have to nursemaid me every minute, you know. There are some things—"

"That you have to do on your own," she finished. "I know. Tia Juanita gave me six kinds of hell for trying to send Pete along."

"Figures," Slocum said with a grin. "Pete told me how you got after him."

He opened the front door for her, and they went inside. Good, spicy smells were starting to emerge from the kitchen, and he said, "Don't you ever cook anymore, Becky?"

Becky snorted and softly smacked his arm. "Not for you, Slocum. Not since that thing you did with my gravy."

Smiling, Slocum shrugged. "I thought it looked kinda nice, what with all them forks and spoons standin' up in it."

"Oh, very funny," she said with a snort. She sat down on the sofa, and taking his hand, drew him down next to her. "So tell me all about it. What happened in town?"

Suddenly, Tia Juanita appeared beside them, and pulled up a rocking chair.

"Yes, Slocum," she said, folding a dish towel in her lap. "What happened? Did you learn anything?"

Some time later, Pete smelled Tia Juanita's cooking when he rode past the main house, and his mouth started to water. It smelled awful good, like peppers and tomatoes and onions and beef.

He wondered if she had made up a pan of those good enchiladas, and if she was going to serve *frijoles* alongside them.

Now, Pete was a refried beans man. He could eat them by the bowlful, topped with lots of that good shredded goat cheese from down home, down at the old Bar S, and plenty of green chili sauce and guacamole. When they had any, that was.

But he wasn't going to see any beans or green chili sauce tonight. Old Fats Harker, the bunkhouse cook, had supplied him—as well as Dave and two other boys—with a cold dinner of biscuits and ham, which they had wrapped in brown paper and tucked into their saddlebags.

They'd see no hot supper tonight, or for the next few days, if he was any judge.

Dave had gone north, Toots had gone south, Baker set out toward the southeast, and now Pete was going east, toward town. Slocum had instructed them to keep watch through the night and alert him if they saw anything funny.

Like, for instance, somebody riding toward the ranch from town.

He'd told them to especially watch for a man in a white-fringed jacket.

Pete didn't know who the man in the fringe was, but he wasn't going to question Slocum. He'd found out three years ago that it just didn't pay.

He rode until he found himself a roost where he could see the road from town pretty well, as well as the surrounding territory. After he settled his horse—and patted his pocket for the fifth time to reassure himself that he hadn't forgotten his pipe—he sat down crosslegged.

Cursing the lack of a fire for coffee-making on what promised to be a bitch of a cold night, he opened up his dinner parcel.

There was a full moon tonight, he thought, chewing as he watched it emerge from the darkening sky, round and large and white. He'd be able to see anything moving on the road for a good ways.

Pete unstoppered his canteen and took a long gulp of water. That Old Harker sure made one holy duster of a dry sandwich. No mustard, no nothing.

He set aside the canteen.

He watched the road.

12

"I think I've got it straight, Slocum," said Becky, from the leather sofa. She sat perched at attention on its edge beside Tia Juanita.

Tia Juanita, the dish towel working absently between her fingers, spoke up. "So, where you say you know this Cassidy from? Is he to be trusted?"

Slocum, standing beside the mantel, nodded. They had lit a fire, for the evening had become a little on the nippy side—as prophesied by Tia Juanita—and the warmth felt good to him. He felt kind of sorry for Pete and the other boys he'd sent out to stand guard. Not sorry enough to join them, though.

He said, "Met him over in Braintree, Texas, about five, maybe six years ago. There was a little range war goin' on back then, and I was hired to help end it. Me and Cassidy started out on opposite sides and ended up workin' together, after I found out my boss was a damn crook."

He smiled. "Kind'a the same as this time, only in reverse. And yes," he added, "I can trust him."

I hope, he thought.

Both women nodded, and then, quite suddenly, Tia Juanita shot to her feet. Slapping a hand to her face, she dashed

89

toward the kitchen, shouting, "Ay! My enchiladas!"

Slocum's brow furrowed. "Hope dinner ain't burnt," he said.

"You," said Becky, rising.

"Me what?"

"Just you," she said, stepping toward him. "After you rode into town and faced both those killers in the saloon—"

"I didn't face nobody, Becky," he cut in.

"You know what I mean. I would have been afraid to even ride into town today."

Smiling, he shook his head. "Now, Becky, I know you. Sooner or later, you'd have taken McMahon's head off."

"No, I wouldn't," she said, pouring out two glasses from the sherry decanter on a side table. She handed him one. "I've changed, Slocum. After so many years of this, well, I guess I'm beaten down."

She took a sip of her sherry, then seemed to reconsider. "I might have poisoned McMahon eventually, or slid a blade between his ribs while he was sleeping, but not before he'd married me."

Suddenly, she downed the glass, as if just the idea of it—either McMahon or the poisoning or the knife, or most probably all three—was incredibly distasteful.

Softly, Slocum said, "I doubt that, honey. Why, you would have run straight for the strychnine before he had a chance to marry you. Or at least, before the wedding night."

Grinning, she smacked his arm and hissed, "Oh, Slocum!"

He chuckled. There was still some fight left in her.

He took a sip of his sherry and looked toward the kitchen. "You suppose supper's about ready? I'm hungry enough to eat a deep-fried horse."

She set her glass down. "Men. Always hungry."

"For one thing or another," he said with a grin, and reached for her.

But she slid away before he could take hold, saying,

"Somebody's got to set the table, and I'm that somebody."
She winked at him, then scampered toward the kitchen.

Slocum stood up and watched her disappear through the
doorway, sighed, then moved to sit in one of the two deep
leather armchairs. It was nice Becky hadn't done anything
to this room. It was all man. Scarred leather chairs and
couches, everything rugged. The only traces of femininity
were the vase of fresh flowers that rode the mantel, and
a smaller vase on the table in back of the big sofa.

The pictures on the walls were likewise masculine.
Horses and cattle, and one of a couple hound dogs. The
one exception hung over the fireplace: a large, stern portrait of the former lord of the manor, Jack Jamison. He
fairly glared out of the painting, as if to say, "This is mine,
goddamnit."

"*Was* yours," Slocum said, and raised his glass to the
late Jack Jamison. "And if we get our way, it's Becky's.
For keeps."

Becky popped through the door again, carrying a stack
of plates, napkins, and a handful of silverware. "What?"
she asked, even though Slocum had little more than mumbled her name.

"Nothin'," said Slocum. He indicated the painting. "Just
talkin' to Jack."

Strangely enough, her mouth quirked up into a hint of
a smile. "It helps me," she said. "It'll help you, too." She
turned toward her work.

Maybe Jack Jamison hadn't been such an old fart after
all, Slocum thought grudgingly.

"I saved them," called Tia Juanita, entering with a
steaming—and enormous—pan of enchiladas. She placed
it on the table, on the towel that Becky had just put down.
The housekeeper motioned to Slocum. "Come. Sit. Eat. I
will get the rest."

Slocum pulled out Becky's chair for her, then sat down
and helped himself to the enchiladas and some extra

cheese. "This is great stuff," he remarked as he took another spoonful.

"Thank you," replied Becky. She shook out her napkin, then paused, looking out the window, into the darkness.

She hugged herself tight. "I wonder how the men are doing out there. It's so cold!"

Teddy LeGrande had slipped out of town with no one the wiser, even that old hack, Cassidy. And what kind of a first name was "Drug" anyway? LeGrande snorted. Now he was slowly making his way due west out the road to the Jamison place.

That Cassidy was really something, wasn't he? The man was plain as an old boot, for one thing. And he was old, for another. LeGrande shook his head and gave another snort. Why, he didn't know how Cassidy could face him again after he'd been outfoxed on the bounty. Hell, LeGrande couldn't even remember the bastard's name—the one he'd turned loose, then shot and turned in for the reward over in Jackson. But he'd bet that Cassidy did.

So when Cassidy told him to lay low for a while, to just bide his time, he figured Cassidy to be playing some sort of game with him. He hadn't figured it out exactly, but it was probably something like Cassidy sneaking out to the S Bar J and gunning Slocum all by himself.

The rat bastard.

He was going to show that Cassidy up, he thought with a smile. Show him up again, more like.

Which was why he was headed toward the S Bar J, long after dark and all by his lonesome. Hell, maybe he'd get to pick up Cassidy's share, too.

And then he mentally kicked himself. He should have asked McMahon about that part.

Well, too late. Come morning, he'd have already killed Slocum and picked up his bounty, and be headed back to

New Mexico. Which would leave behind a real big—and real unpleasant—surprise for Cassidy.

He grinned at that one.

This Slocum was all reputation. He'd heard of him, sure. But he'd also heard about a lot of men who were supposed to be fast or slick or cunning, or all three. The last one of those big-reputation guns that he'd run across was the Arapaho Kid, who happened to be all of sixteen years old.

LeGrande had tracked him to the bath house in Trestle Junction, New Mexico, and shot him while he was in the tub. He'd left the kid floating, facedown in the dirty water.

Some shootist.

But Perry Broadside, the man who'd contracted the killing—having listened to those stories about the Arapaho Kid, and wanting rid of anyone who could possibly cause his horse rustling operation any trouble—had paid him anyway, boy or not.

That was the kind of client LeGrande liked. No questions, just pay the money.

Tate McMahon struck him as that sort.

LeGrande figured Slocum wouldn't suspect he was coming. Hell, the man hadn't set foot into town, not once! He was probably already scared out of his britches. Probably quivering in his boots!

He'd never suspect Teddy LeGrande was coming to call . . . and blow him to Kingdom Come.

The moon was bright and the road was clear. He began to whistle.

This would be about the easiest five hundred he'd made all year.

Pete was colder than the balls on a brass monkey. At least, that was what he thought as he sat there, shivering while he watched the road. He knew there was a blanket tied behind his saddle, but somehow, the idea of moving—

and thus exposing a few new parts of himself to the weather—held little appeal.

Tia Juanita had been right when she insisted that the men take blankets to wrap themselves in. Hell, she was always right. And somehow, she knew every damned thing that happened on that spread. She must have had a few of those Mexican witches in her family, that's what he thought.

Brujas. Anyhow, that was what he thought they called them.

When he found he was too cold even to lift a jittering hand to reach into his pocket and check his watch, he gritted his teeth and stood up as fast as his cold and creaky bones could travel.

As he had expected, this plunge into an icy stream of air was all the motive he needed to hustle over the rise to where he'd left his rig and snatch up the blanket. Hurriedly, he shook it out and wrapped it around his shoulders.

Better. But he tramped around for a few minutes, stamping his feet and getting his joints oiled up and half-way warm again before he sat down.

Damn! he thought as he settled once again. Why couldn't there have been a rock or something out here that he could cuddle up to?

The land was softly rolling around this part of the ranch. Pete had hobbled his gelding down in the soft hollow behind him so that he couldn't be seen, just in case anybody did come down that road. But Pete just sat there, as obvious as a sore thumb.

If I'd a thought about it, he mused, *I would'a brung my own boulder . . .*

He had just got the blanket tucked into every available nook and cranny when he suddenly leaned forward, squinted, and froze.

"That ain't no bird," he whispered. The whistling was a little louder now. He could hear it faintly, but steadily.

He still couldn't see anything, though. And if he couldn't see the whistler, then the whistler couldn't see him. Yet.

As quickly as he could, he shrugged free of the blanket and flattened pressing his belly to the ground. He brought his rifle up and rested his cheek against the stock.

There! There he was. Pete could just make out a faint shape moving toward him.

A faint shape in a pale jacket, riding a pale horse, maybe a palomino.

It was just like Slocum had said, and for just a second, Pete wondered if maybe Slocum wasn't related to Tia Juanita and all those witches.

The rider came closer, preceded by the sound of his whistling, and Pete found that he was sweating despite the cold. It beaded on his forehead and trickled down his nose.

Of course, he wasn't supposed to shoot the fellow. He was only supposed to report back.

But the whistler was almost in range—the range that Pete felt safe with, when it was dark and he couldn't see too well. He couldn't stand up now without giving himself away.

He decided to wait until the man passed, then sneak around him, go back to the ranch, and get Slocum.

But then the man in the white jacket reined up his horse and just sat there, square in the middle of the road.

Pete screwed up his face. "What the—" he muttered before he realized that the sonofabitch had seen the barrel of his rifle, glinting in the moonlight.

Damn it, anyway!

The man shifted, like he was reaching for his rifle.

Pete reacted immediately. He fired—and missed.

Cursing, he took careful aim—trying not to think about the rifle that the man out there was just bringing to his shoulder—and fired again.

This time, the figure on the horse wavered a split second after Pete pulled the trigger.

But he didn't fall off his damned horse. No, he *got* off, dismounted fast but deliberately on the horse's off side, and began to return fire.

He was sloppy about it though. Pete could hear his slugs sharply drilling the dirt about ten feet in front of him and to the right.

He aimed again.

This time, the man, who was halfway into the brush beside the road, screamed, stood straight, then fell over.

Pete didn't move, though. Watching intently for the slightest movement of brush, he waited a good fifteen minutes. Then he began to creep slowly toward the site, sometimes on his hands and knees, sometimes in a crouch.

He cut up to the north a mite before he closed in, his handgun drawn and ready. He moved slowly, quietly, and with his heart thumping a mile a minute.

He finally found the body, down in the brush, by nearly falling over it. But he caught himself and, holding his breath, toed the man's shoulder.

No response.

Letting out a relieved sigh that rose up in a foggy plume, Pete relaxed. He stuck his boot out again, and this time rolled the body over. Just as he was thinking that this fellow moved awful easy for a big, dead man, he saw the man's hand move, heard the blast of a gun, and felt searing heat in his shoulder.

He fired even as his body was shoved back by the impact, and the body on the ground convulsed once, then lay still.

Pete managed not to fall down, but he cussed up a storm as he stumbled. Catching himself, he fired into the body again, just to make certain the bastard was dead.

"Sonofabitch!" he spat as he slowly walked up to the road to snag the fellow's mount.

"Now I gotta load you clear up on that big yaller horse, and me with a stove-up shoulder!"

13

Cassidy swore under his breath.

Snuck out! That goddamn LeGrande had snuck out on him! He'd snuck clear out of town, too, insofar as Cassidy could tell. At least, his horse wasn't here, in the livery.

Oh, LeGrande'd had him going, all right. Or more like, he'd had himself going. Cassidy had thought that maybe he'd seen a glimmer of something in there, behind those eyes. That maybe LeGrande did have something on the ball, and that nobody could be that dumb on purpose. But he'd been wrong.

Anything crafty that dwelt inside LeGrande's brain was just more stupidity.

Sonofabitch!

"When'd he leave?" he snapped at the perplexed hostler, who, by the looks of him, was just getting ready for bed. At least, he was halfway into his nightclothes, and through the door to what Cassidy had thought was a feed room sat a cot with the bedding turned down. A glowing lantern was perched on the overturned barrel beside it.

"Who?" asked the hostler angrily. He was a little man, shorter than Cassidy by half a head, no bigger around than a coiled lariat, and balding on top. "I don't keep track of

97

everybody what comes and goes, y' know."

"The man who left a big palomino gelding in here to-day," Cassidy snapped back. LeGrande had told him about the horse while they were in the bar and LeGrande was trying to impress him.

It figured he'd ride a palomino. Probably a goddamn parade horse.

"Oh, him," the hostler said, scratching the stubble on his chin. "He come in 'bout an hour, hour and a quarter ago, I reckon. Big galoot in one'a them white, fringified jackets, right?"

Cassidy nodded.

"Thought they made them things up for the dime novels," the hostler mused. "Never see'd one in real life afore."

Cassidy had a short, silent debate with himself. Should he follow LeGrande? Cassidy knew exactly where he was going. On the other hand, Slocum would be prepared. There was nothing Cassidy could do out at the S Bar J except turn up unexpectedly and get himself shot.

Accidentally, of course, but he'd still be shot.

The proposition didn't hold much appeal.

At last, he reluctantly decided that he'd do the most good where he and Slocum had agreed—in town, with his eye firmly on Tate McMahon.

The hostler was staring at him impatiently with beady little blue eyes. "Well?" he demanded. "That all you want, Mister?"

"Yeah," said Cassidy, heading for the door. "That's all."

It was getting nippy, he thought as he walked back toward the hotel, and he snugged his jacket tighter and buttoned it up. He didn't care for the cold.

And then he felt sorry—very briefly—for Teddy LeGrande.

It was a bad night to die.

• • •

Tate McMahon lived at the McMahon Hotel, which he also happened to own. A year back, he had knocked out several walls and made himself a suite of what had formerly been the biggest room in the place, and two smaller ones. He ended up with a bedroom, a sitting room, and a big parlor with a fireplace. He liked them just fine.

Right at the moment, he was slouched in one of the large, wingback chairs that faced his fireplace, staring into the flames. And thinking.

He supposed he'd need to call LeGrande and Cassidy into the office tomorrow. He'd ask them what they were going to do, if anything. Frankly, he was surprised they hadn't ridden out to the S Bar J directly after their meeting.

And frankly, he was disappointed.

"I should have just gone to the source," he muttered aloud. But bringing Jeb Crowfoot back to Indian Springs was just about the last thing he wanted to do.

For one thing, he was fairly sure that Crowfoot would be just as likely to shoot him—or anybody unlucky enough to pass him on the street and cough at an inopportune moment—as shoot somebody else on the S Bar J.

Oh, Crowfoot was good all right. The best! And he was an unknown face, a little-mentioned name. He was as expensive as hell, though, and hard to track down, let alone convince to travel for a job. He headquartered in San Francisco, but he was apt to be anywhere—except where he'd previously done a job.

Crowfoot thought it was bad luck. Of course, he was one crazy bastard, about two steps away from the looney bin. McMahon had only seen him for five minutes before—and two minutes after—he'd shot Jack Jamison. Crowfoot always wore gloves, and McMahon would bet good money that he had checked his watch and folded and refolded his handkerchief ten times in those seven minutes.

He'd straightened McMahon's desktop, too, and threatened him with a sleeve gun when he handed over money that wasn't in a cloth pouch. Well, how was he to know the bastard didn't touch things that he hadn't boiled first?

He'd had to borrow a little bag from Siddons, who then spent the rest of the day complaining that her mirror—which had been the former occupant of said pouch—was going to get scratched in her handbag.

McMahon snorted. As if looking in a mirror would help her face any.

Besides having a quick temper—and the talent with both gun and rifle to do something about it—Crowfoot just plain gave him the heebie-geebies.

He leaned forward, tipped the fireplace poker into his hand, and stabbed at the logs, turning over the topmost one. The fire blazed up momentarily.

He stared deep into the flames. And then he smiled.

So what if they hadn't got going yet, if they were a little hesitant? He supposed he would be, too, if he were called to a strange town to kill someone he'd never met, someone whose status was unknown. He supposed he'd been a little unfair, too, expecting them to just charge on out there.

After all, they didn't know Slocum on sight. As far as they were concerned, he was a wild card. They couldn't be certain that he wasn't out there raising a goddamn army.

McMahon snickered under his breath. "An army? Oh, that's good!"

The S Bar J had only about a dozen hands. Plus, if Slocum was too much of a coward to come into town and seek him out, he'd probably already fled the damned county.

Laughing again, this time more jovially, he put away

the poker and leaned back, slumping in his chair. He unbuttoned his vest and sighed deeply with satisfaction.

Tomorrow. Tomorrow he'd talk to Cassidy and Le-Grande. Maybe he'd start a little competition between the two of them. He'd tell them that the man who actually killed Slocum got a two-hundred-dollar bonus or something—and the man who came up empty-handed? He left empty-handed. Zilch, nada, nothing. It would light a fire under their lazy asses, give them an incentive.

Yes, he thought, picking up his bourbon. That would be perfect.

Slocum and Becky lay panting in each other's arms, tangled in a sea of legs and arms and soft green quilt. Becky snuggled closer to his chest, gave the quilt a tug to cover her shoulder, and whispered, "I wish you could stay."

The sentence addled Slocum a little, since he wasn't expecting her to say it—or at least, say it out loud. But he recovered in a split second and gave her a hug. "Becky," he began, "I—"

He never got to finish, because suddenly Becky bolted upright and stared past him, out the window. "What in heaven's name?" she muttered.

Pulling the quilt off him and wrapping it around herself, she rose and stepped over him, then down off the bed.

Suddenly freezing, Slocum grabbed a sheet while she opened the window.

"Pete?" she called out into the darkness. "Pete? Is that you?"

Slocum swung his legs over the side of the bed and yanked the sheet along. Damn it anyway! He was just getting in the mood for a second go around.

As Slocum stumbled of the sheet, then caught himself, he heard Pete call, "Yes'm." Joining Becky, he saw murky figures in the yard, which came closer, then crystalized into two horses. And one slouching rider.

A second later, he realized there was a body slung over the second horse.

"Sonofabitch," he muttered, reaching for his britches.

"What happened?" Becky called.

Thinly, he heard Pete reply, "Tell Slocum I shot that feller. Sorry."

His pants and gunbelt on, Slocum tugged on his boots.

"Is Pete all right?" he asked.

But at the same moment, Pete said, "Miss Becky? I'm kind'a bleedin', here."

Slocum didn't bother to button his shirt. His shirt tails flapping, he moved Becky aside and swung himself right out the window.

Becky didn't say a word. The last thing he saw before he went out to Pete was Becky, dropping that quilt and grabbing for her robe.

Pete wasn't in any condition to spy on her, even if he'd been at the right angle. He sat weaving on his horse, as if, having used the last of his strength to get back to the ranch, he figured it was now safe to die.

"Fat chance of that, old buddy," Slocum muttered, practically reading Pete's mind as the hand blacked out and fell off his horse, straight into Slocum's arms. For the moment, Slocum let him slide gently to the ground. Then he rounded Pete's horse to check on the body.

It was LeGrande, all right. Somehow, he'd got past Cassidy at the hotel. He'd likely decided to ride out and kill Slocum himself.

Well, guess what? Slocum thought as he lifted Le-Grande's head by his yellow hair and took another look at his face. "You got yourself a little surprise, didn't you, bounty hunter?"

Slocum used the phrase loosely, but then he didn't like to speak ill of the dead, even if the deceased was a lame-brained showoff of a killer.

He let LeGrande's head drop, pulled down his horse's

reins, then bent to Pete. There was a lot of blood, but it looked like it had all come from a shoulder wound. It was patchable, Slocum decided with a grunt.

"Pete?" he said, lightly slapping the foreman's cheek. "Dammit, wake up!"

Pete groaned.

"Atta boy," Slocum said. "On your feet and into the house."

He got Pete up and on his feet, even though Pete was only semiconscious. The horses and LeGrande's body trailing behind, Slocum helped him slowly toward the front of the house.

Becky—in a pale blue robe, her hair pulled back with a simple ribbon and her cheeks pink with the cold—met them at the corner of the porch and propped up Pete's other side.

"Is it bad?" she asked Slocum, and her voice was full of worry.

"He'll live," Slocum replied as they rounded the corner.

"Who's that?" With her head, Becky motioned toward the body.

"Teddy LeGrande," Slocum said. "Big surprise, ain't it?"

Becky snorted, then stopped. Slocum stopped, too. She said, "This really messes up your plans, doesn't it? I mean, yours and Mr. Cassidy's."

"Yeah," was all he said.

As they mounted the porch steps, Tia Juanita came out the front door, yawning and tugging her robe closer about her.

"What are you people doing out here?" she asked, and then she saw Pete. Crossing herself swiftly, she rushed across the porch, pushed Becky aside, and practically hefted Pete into her arms. *"Dios mio!"* she cried, and dragged Pete into the house singlehandedly.

Which left Becky and Slocum alone on the porch.

They looked at each other for moment, not saying anything, not having to say anything.

"Becky!" called Tia Juanita from inside the house.

"Coming," Becky said. She tore her eyes away from Slocum's, turned, and went through the door.

Slocum walked slowly down the steps and toward the waiting horses. He led them, with LeGrande's body, down to the barn.

14

Slocum laid Teddy LeGrande out in an empty stall, then stripped and rubbed down the horses. Pete's bay went into the corral, but LeGrande's flashy palomino stayed in the barn, where he couldn't be seen by curious eyes.

Pete had killed Teddy LeGrande, all right, but he'd sure taken his own sweet time about it. LeGrande had been shot once in his left lung and once through his upper arm. Judging by the amount of blood that had come from those two wounds—and decorated LeGrande's white leather jacket—they hadn't killed him.

The other two wounds were straight through the heart. One had bled a little; the other one, not at all.

Slocum had constructed a pretty fair scenario of what had happened before, he once again climbed the porch steps to the house.

Pete was half-lying, half-sitting on the smaller leather couch. His jacket and shirt were off, exposing his pasty-white chest, and both women were buzzing around him—and fussing over him—like bees at a bed of spring flowers.

"Get the slug out?" Slocum asked as he closed the door behind him. His shirt was still flapping and he was colder than all get out. Directly, he went to the fire and threw another log atop it.

"No need," said Tia Juanita.

"It went through," added Becky, busy with bandages. "We found it just inside his coat, halfway through the wool. Darnedest thing I've ever seen."

Pete, who was sipping on what looked like a bourbon, smiled lopsidedly, and held up a slightly misshapen slug.

"Souvenir," Pete said, then yelped when Becky tried to move him forward just a tad.

"Honestly, you big baby," Becky scolded, although her voice was full of relief. "Hold still."

"You mind her, Pete," Tia Juanita said as she gathered up the pan of water and bloody rags. She carried them to the kitchen.

"You want a report, Slocum?" Pete asked, still wincing. He took another big sip of his whiskey.

Slocum slouched into a chair and put his boots up on the ottoman. "You shot LeGrande. Shot him twice." He dug into the humidor by his chair and pulled out a cigar. "You waited awhile, then snuck up to make sure he wasn't playin' possum. Which he was."

Slocum flicked a lucifer into flame and lit his cigar. "You fired point-blank, and a few seconds later, you fired point-blank again," he continued. "I'm guessin' that he clipped you between the first two and the last two shots. How'm I doin'?"

"Hell, I don't know why I bothered to come back," Pete growled as Becky stood back and surveyed her work. "Can I get somethin' to cover me?" he asked Becky. "I feel naked as a jaybird."

"Surely, Pete," she replied. "I'll fetch you a blanket." Throwing a look backward that Slocum couldn't read, she went down the hall.

"I take that means I'm right," Slocum said. He got up and crossed the room, found the whiskey amid the other decanters, and poured himself a shot. "Damn, it's cold out there!"

"Not cold enough to snow," mused Pete absently. The whiskey was beginning to take hold. "But darn near." He studied the bottom of his empty glass, then held it out.

Slocum rolled his eyes, but took it. After pouring out a generous refill—Pete was still white as a ghost—he handed it back.

"Thanks," said Pete, and downed half of it.

"Go slow on that," Slocum warned as he sat down again.

"Soon as I get my innards warmed up decent," the foreman replied. "You put up my horse?"

"Yeah," Slocum said just as Becky bustled back into the parlor, carrying a worn but soft-looking Navajo blanket.

She draped it gently over Pete's shoulders and tucked it in a bit, then said, "You're not going back out to the bunkhouse, Pete. You're staying here, in the spare room, until you're better."

With a pained expression, Pete whined, "Do I gotta?"

Slocum was about to say the same thing. Pete was going to be all right, and the last thing Slocum needed—or wanted—was a big pair of ears on the other side of Becky's bedroom wall.

They sometimes disturbed Tia Juanita, and her room was on the other end of the house!

But in a firm voice, Becky said, "You're staying up at the house, Pete. For at least tonight." When Pete opened his mouth to protest, she said, "I mean it. No arguments!"

Pete let out a weary sigh.

Slocum did, as well, although his was more in frustration. He guessed that put the cap on any more loving tonight. Damn it.

Tia Juanita came back in from the kitchen. Having obviously overheard the preceding conversation, she went to Pete and said, "Can you stand up?"

Pete allowed that he could, although the actuality of it was accompanied by a great deal of help from the housekeeper, and a lot of whines, whimpers, and groans on his part.

Pete made a grab for his whiskey glass at the last minute, but Tia Juanita said, "You touch that again, I will poke your shoulder on purpose. You have had enough."

"Yes, ma'am," Pete said sheepishly. She led him from the room.

In silence, Becky poured herself a whiskey and took a long, thoughtful sip. Sighing, she looked across the room at Slocum, and locked eyes with him. She said, "We're in a lot of trouble, aren't we?"

Frowning around his cigar, Slocum grunted. "Looks like."

The next morning, Cassidy came downstairs to find a note, left with the desk clerk, that read, *"Mr. Cassidy, Please be in my office at nine o'clock sharp."* It was signed, *"Tate McMahon, Esq."*

Cassidy snorted at that "esquire" bit. Who did McMahon think he was fooling, anyway. He crumpled the note in his hand, and when the desk clerk was distracted by someone asking what time the stage to Prescott would be through, he had a good look at the hotel's mail slots.

McMahon had left a note in LeGrande's box, too. Same kind of paper, same size.

It was apparent, then, that McMahon didn't know that last night, LeGrande had left the hotel and scooted out of town. If he did, he'd also know that LeGrande was never coming back to Indian Springs; at least, not in the condition in which he'd left it.

Cassidy located the wastebasket and tossed his crumpled note into it, then walked out the front doors. He went down the street to the Hummingbird Café—which he guessed McMahon didn't own, since his name wasn't plastered all over it—and ordered himself a big plate of eggs, bacon, hash browns, and sausage.

He had an hour before he had to go up to McMahon's and act surprised when LeGrande didn't show up. Keeping a watchful eye on the front window and the street outside, he tucked the napkin into his collar, picked up a fork, and dug into his breakfast.

"What are we going to do with him?" Becky asked.

Despite Slocum's warnings, she had insisted on walking down to the barn to view the body. They stood outside the stall where Dave knelt beside the body.

"Bury him, I reckon," Slocum said.

"Not beside Jack, you won't," she said firmly.

This startled Slocum a little, although he realized that it shouldn't. Still, why was he taking everything so personally when it had to do with Becky Jamison and her late husband?

By the time Becky looked over at him, his face was stone and he said, "We can take him out on the range, then."

"Fine," Becky said. "And don't mark it," she added before she turned on her heel.

Slocum said to Dave, "You heard the lady," then went to join her.

As they walked up to the house she snapped, "Honestly, Slocum!"

"What?"

"How could you think of planting a man like that killer next to Jack? For all I know, LeGrande killed my husband!"

Slocum reached out and grabbed her arm, pulling her to a halt. "We'll bury him wherever you say, Becky," he said. "But LeGrande wasn't the killer."

"And how do you know that?"

"Because I checked his rifle and his cartridge belt. All plain casings. The man we're lookin' for—"

"Marks his with a puma," she said, cutting him off. "I know. You told me. But how do you know for sure that it wasn't just some sort of a lark with LeGrande? What if he did it then, but now he doesn't?"

He scratched the back of his head. He hadn't thought of that. On further consideration, though, he said, "Don't seem likely, Becky."

"I still don't want him buried anywhere near my house," she insisted, and began to walk again.

Slocum stayed where he stood, watching as she stomped toward the house and up the porch steps. When Becky got like this, well, he knew to just stand back and let her thrash. She'd calm down all by herself, and in her own time.

He walked out to the far end of the corral, Concho dogging his steps along the other side of the fence. Patting the horse on the neck, he muttered, "At least you're always the same."

He looked east, in the direction of Indian Springs saying softly, "Wish I knew what was goin' on with Cassidy."

"Well?" McMahon demanded.

Cassidy, who had just walked into McMahon's office for the second time that morning, perched lazily on the edge of the desk and said, "That big yellow of his is still gone. Figured this would happen when I found him took-off last night, the big, dumb sonofabitch." He shook his head.

"I ought to fire your worthless ass, too!" McMahon shouted. Things weren't going his way at all, and he had to holler at somebody. Cassidy was handy.

"You didn't fire Teddy LeGrande," replied Cassidy,

idly picking at a thread on his knee. "I reckon he sort of fired his own self."

"You know what I mean!" McMahon stormed. He found himself on his feet, found his hands balled up into fists. "Why didn't you let me know what was going on? You're supposed to be working for me!"

Cassidy, apparently unimpressed, shrugged. "It was late. Didn't want to bother you. Besides, what were you gonna do? Send out the goddamn cavalry or somethin'?"

McMahon went to the window and stood there a moment, simmering. However maddening he might be, Cassidy was right. What could he have done in the dark of night? Besides, Cassidy might not have considered all the possibilities. Why, LeGrande might have been scared off by all the Slocum stories and just plain run out on them! Yes, that was more probable.

Suddenly, McMahon wheeled toward Cassidy.

"He's tucked his tail," he announced to Cassidy, who just cocked a brow.

Cassidy pursed his lips and nodded. "Maybe so," came the reply. "Mayhap he lit out. Didn't consider that."

"I'll bet you didn't," McMahon said curtly, and went back behind his desk. He signaled to Cassidy to get the hell off his desk—which he did, albeit slowly—then slid out a piece of stationery.

He should have done this in the first place, he thought as he scribbled out the message. He blotted the ink, then folded the paper. He handed it to Cassidy.

"Take that to the telegraph office," he said.

Cassidy didn't accept the paper, though. He just stood there, frowning. "What? I'm your errand boy, now? Seems to me you hired me for a whole different kind of job."

"I did," snapped McMahon. "But if you don't want to be fired, you'll go send that wire. It's my suspicion that Slocum's reputation is what caused our Mr. LeGrande to leave in the middle of the night. Perhaps it's true. Perhaps only half of it's true. But I want two men on my side."

He looked Cassidy up and down. "Perhaps just one and a half," he said, sniffing.

Cassidy, expressionless, snatched the paper from his hand, then nodded.

"Anything you say, boss," he said.

Cassidy walked until he knew he was out of McMahon's sight, then stepped into the mouth of an alley.

"A man and a half my aunt Betty, you shiny, slicked-up sonofabitch," he muttered as he unfolded the paper. He held it at arm's length and squinted.

The proposed wire was addressed to somebody named Jeb Crowfoot in San Francisco, and the message included a "Please Forward." The rest of the message was filled up with telling Crowfoot that McMahon had a job for him—and telling the telegrapher to put the wire on McMahon's bill.

"Hell!" Cassidy muttered, in the throes of a new surge of disgust. "He's payin' this Crowfoot a thousand!"

His first inclination was to simply crumple the paper and forget he'd ever seen it. But then, maybe this Crowfoot would prove interesting. He'd sure buy them some time, having to come from San Francisco and all.

Carefully, Cassidy refolded the paper and stuck it into his breast pocket.

He'd send McMahon's damned telegram, he thought, stepping back up on the boardwalk.

And then he'd take himself a little ride out west of town to see old Slocum.

15

"He's callin' in somebody named Jeb Crowfoot," Cassidy said. Behind him, through the open doorway, Slocum could see a neatly put together but plain bay gelding tied to the porch rail. Cassidy handed his hat to Tia Juanita. "Thank you, ma'am."

The housekeeper pointed to his boots. "No spurs in this house," she said firmly before she hung his hat on a peg by the door and went down the hall, presumably to clean something.

"She always like that?" Cassidy asked.

"Yeah," Slocum replied, glad to see that Tia Juanita's bossy attitude wasn't reserved just for folks she already knew. "And no," he added with a smile before Cassidy could ask the question, "she ain't the one."

Cassidy returned the grin. "That's a relief." He sat down at the table and obediently took off his spurs, then slung them up on the table with a clink and a jangle. He looked around him. "Nice roost you fell into, Slocum. Real nice." His gaze fell on the portrait above the mantel. "Who's the character in the painting?"

"Former owner," Slocum said without further explanation. He pulled out a chair, turned it around, and sat down with his arms draped over the back. "So, who's this Jeb Crowfoot feller? You know anything about him?"

Cassidy shrugged. "You got me."

Slocum's brow furrowed. "Seems to me I heard somethin' or other, but I guess it wasn't important enough to stick to my brain." He shook his head. "I'm drawin' a blank."

"Back to square one," said Cassidy, rubbing his neck. "What beats me, Slocum, is why the sonofabitch wants these ranches, anyhow. Can't see that he's doin' anything with 'em. There's no point to it, unless he just wants to be king of his own little country or somethin'. The part of it that's flat is only fair grazing land, and the other half's too up-and-down and goddamned rocky for anything. 'Cept maybe raisin' horny toads and diamondbacks."

"Unless . . ." Slocum stared off into the distance, thinking. Something was brewing at the back of his brain, but he couldn't quite get a handle on the pot.

The screen door banged, and both men looked toward it.

It was Becky, just coming back from the old Bar S, her arms full of sacks filled with goat cheese. The sunlight from behind her lit her with a kind of halo, and for a second, Slocum went all mushy inside. Then she took a step into the house, and it was gone.

She still looked mighty good, though.

She smiled and said, "It's surely warm out, considering how chilly it was last night. How's Pete?"

"Up and walkin', and gone down to the bunkhouse," Slocum said. "Those three hands I sent with you look after you all right?"

Before she had time to answer, Cassidy got to his feet, whispering, "Nice goin'," and said, more loudly, "Ma'am."

Still seated, Slocum said, "Sorry. Becky, honey, this here's Drug Cassidy."

Becky stepped right up, shifted both bags to her other arm, and extended her hand. "Delighted, Mr. Cassidy. I've heard a great deal about you."

Cassidy took it. "Yes, ma'am. Likewise. I mean," he hastily added, "I ain't heard all that much about . . . I mean . . . Aw, hell."

Becky, bless her heart, laughed, and Cassidy flushed. "That's all right, Mr. Cassidy. I think I know what you meant to say." She turned toward Slocum and announced, "I'll be back in a minute. And no, thank you, I don't need any help with these parcels."

Chagrined, Slocum belatedly jumped to his feet and was reaching out for the sacks when he collided with Drug Cassidy, who was trying to do the same thing. Becky slipped away, chuckling softly, and went into the kitchen.

Which left Slocum to ease back down in his chair. Cassidy was still standing, though, staring after Becky, his mouth agape.

Slocum frowned. "What the hell's wrong with you, Drug?"

Cassidy, never taking his eyes from the now-vacant kitchen doorway, whispered, "Good glory, Slocum! I do believe she's the prettiest little thing I ever did see."

Slocum's chest swelled with pride, but Cassidy wasn't looking his way. Just as quick as he'd puffed up, Slocum went flat.

"She's taken, Drug," he said curtly.

Cassidy seemed to get control of himself, and returned to his chair. Sheepishly, he managed a weak grin. "Sorry," he said. "Didn't mean nothin' by it."

Without smiling, Slocum grunted and said, "S'all right. So, it's gonna take a few days for this Crowfoot to show up. If he does. In the meantime, I got sort of a hunch what McMahon might be up to."

Cassidy leaned forward. "What's that?"

Slocum shook his head. "Right now, it's just a hunch."

Just then, Becky came in from the kitchen, bearing a tray. "Limeade, gentlemen? Or coffee? There's pecan pie, too."

Late that afternoon, Tate McMahon was just locking up his office when a shadow fell over him. Thinking it was Siddons, come back because she'd left something or other behind in the office—which she was wont to do—he muttered, "Forget your handbag again?" before he turned around.

But it wasn't Siddons.

Big as life, wearing a tidy outfit consisting of a starched white shirt, tan britches with a knife's edge crease, a sleek deerhide jacket—sans any fringe—and boots without a spec of dust on them, stood Jeb Crowfoot.

McMahon actually jumped. If he hadn't grabbed the doorknob, he would have fallen all the way down.

"Wha-wha-what?" was all he managed to get out.

"You sent for me," came the deep, resonant voice. Although Crowfoot spoke perfect English and wore white mens' clothes, it was obvious he was Indian, or at least, part Indian. McMahon didn't know what tribe—or tribes—had produced him, or where he'd come from. He didn't much care.

He straightened, gave his vest a tug, and said, "How'd you get here so quick?"

Any way you looked at it, San Francisco, California, was a long haul from Indian Springs, Arizona. Although, quite frankly, if Crowfoot told him that he'd summoned up the god of wind to carry him aloft, McMahon would have been inclined to believe him.

But Crowfoot, who kept his distance and kept his gloved hands at his sides, said, "I have an assistant in San Francisco. He forwarded me your message." He paused a moment, then added, "I was over in Prescott. On business."

"That's still awful damn fast," McMahon said.

Crowfoot scowled, as if McMahon was a blithering idiot. He said, "You mentioned a thousand dollars."

"Yes, yes, I did," McMahon said, then belatedly realized they were standing on the street where they could be seen by any passerby. Hurriedly, he fumbled for the key, stuck it in the lock, and opened the door. "Come in, come in," he said. All his words seemed to be coming in doubles.

He was a little afraid of Crowfoot.

All right, he was afraid, period. The man was an Indian, all his white-man's trappings to the contrary, and on top of that, he was crazy. A crazy Indian. What had he been thinking when he sent for him again?

Crowfoot stepped in and, with the tip of his boot heel, closed the door behind them.

"It had better be a thousand," Crowfoot said. He looked as though a smile had never crossed his face. "I'm making an exception. I don't like to visit the same town twice."

McMahon swallowed. "Yes, I know," he said, sounding a great deal calmer than he felt. "That's why I doubled your price."

Crowfoot just stared at him.

"I had two hired guns," McMahon continued, unable to stop himself. "Teddy LeGrande and Drug Cassidy."

Crowfoot sniffed derisively and said, "LeGrande. Ha!"

"He rode out," continued McMahon. "Scared off, I guess. Cassidy's still here."

"Why?"

The question was so blunt that it took McMahon aback. However, he recovered quickly. "I'm not sure, now that you mention it. I won't need him now, I suppose."

"Who do you want me to kill?"

Again, no bones about it. Crowfoot was as subtle as an oncoming locomotive.

"A man named Slocum. Heard of him?"

Crowfoot didn't flinch, nor did he relax. Still totally without expression, he nodded curtly, saying, "I've heard things."

McMahon would've liked to ask just exactly what Crowfoot had heard, but he was anxious to get the man out of his office as soon as possible. He shifted his weight to the other foot.

"He's staying out at the S Bar J."

"Same as last time?"

"Same as last time."

"Picture?"

"No," said McMahon. "But he's tall, about six-one, six-two. Dark hair, more rugged than handsome. My boys tell me he always rides—"

"An Appaloosa," Crowfoot cut in. "I know."

McMahon wondered how he knew, but once again, he didn't ask.

"I'll do it tomorrow," Crowfoot said. "Have the money ready. And this time, boil it first."

"Surely," said McMahon, nodding like an idiot.

Crowfoot looked at the doorknob, then looked at McMahon.

McMahon hurried to open the door, then watched while Crowfoot stepped through it and walked down the street. He mounted a sorrel horse, flecked with a little white on its rump and tied in front of the McMahon Dry Goods. Slowly, he jogged down the street.

McMahon heaved a sigh. Thank God that was over with. Crowfoot made his skin crawl.

But Crowfoot would get the job done quickly and efficiently. Of this, he was certain.

And McMahon was also certain that he'd go into the bank the first thing in the morning and withdraw a thousand dollars in gold coins, boil the damned stuff, and put it neatly into a tidy cloth pouch. Which he wouldn't borrow from Siddons this time. The notions store had them. He'd asked.

Crowfoot was out of sight, by this time. He wouldn't stay in the hotel. He wouldn't even stay in town. At least, he hadn't the last time. The man was just plain spooky. Wouldn't touch anything. McMahon wondered if he boiled his blasted horse before he rode him.

Snorting, he stepped outside and locked the door behind him again. Perhaps he'd stop up at the notions store now. Mildred wouldn't have closed quite yet. And then he'd go back to the hotel and have a little talk with Mr. Drug Cassidy. Tell him he was no longer needed.

As he made his way up the street, he considered that he'd only have to see Crowfoot one more time, to pay him off. And by then, all his other troubles would be in the past. No more Slocum, no more Crowfoot—who would be loathe to ever show his face in Indian Springs again—and, in short order, he'd have Becky Jamison's hand in marriage.

He'd have the rest of her, too, he thought with a quick grin. Most importantly, though, he'd have her land. And everything in it.

16

After riding a few miles from town, Jeb Crowfoot found an area forlorn enough to meet his standards, and stopped to make camp for the night. There was never any question that he might stay in town. No filthy hotel beds for him. He preferred his saddle for a pillow and his own blankets, laid upon the relatively grime-free soil. Free of human grime, that was.

First, he took a fresh, white handkerchief from the wrapped bundle in his saddlebag, and tied it over his face to prevent the inhaling of any more dust than necessary. Then, he thoroughly curried and brushed his horse, picking out its hooves and combing its mane and tail thoroughly before wiping it down with a clean, soft cloth. He refolded the cloth, dirty side in, wrapped it in the handkerchief he'd tied over his nose and mouth, and placed them inside the other saddlebags. The curry comb and brush, he fastidiously and laboriously cleaned on the leaves of a nearby plant before he wrapped them in a scrap of chamois and put them away. That done, he set to making his camp. He made a small fire: the kindling, in even numbers, neatly arranged. He got out his spotless coffeepot and filled it and started it to boil, and then un-

121

wrapped the jackrabbit he'd shot on the way out from Indian Springs.

He skinned and cleaned it, cut it into pieces and put it in a frying pan. And then he set to making a bed.

His bedroll was placed on the cleanest, most even spot of ground he could find, which he swept free of every last pebble. After the blankets were neatly rolled out and patted free of creases, he placed his saddle at its head, the stirrups arranged just so. His rifle went neatly alongside the bedding.

At last, he sat down.

While his coffee heated and his jackrabbit fried, he pulled a dull nail from his pocket and from his belt, two new cartridges—one for the kill shot, and one just to make certain.

He then began, laboriously, to *tap-tap-tap* the tiny head of a cougar into each casing.

Drugman Cassidy had no more than gotten comfortable in his room when a knock came on the door. "Go away," he shouted from the bed. He figured to take himself a little nap and rest his eyes, then go down for a late supper.

But a voice from the hallway called, "Mr. Cassidy, sir? Mr. McMahon would like you to have supper with him. In fifteen minutes, downstairs?"

Cassidy sighed. Goddamnit, anyway.

Without opening his eyes, he shouted back, "Okay. Fifteen minutes." He heard footsteps going away, down the hall.

His eyes had bothered him more and more this past year. Not just the seeing out of them, either. It seemed like lately they always felt full of grit or something. He'd given up on washing them out, or at least, trying to wash the grit out.

He'd grown to accept it. That was just the way it was. But they were worse on days when he'd spent a long time out in the wind, or even just plain outside. For the past year, he'd stayed mostly in his hotel room back home, except when he had a job. That had been exactly twice.

He had really needed this five hundred that McMahon had offered. It would put his retirement fund over the top, and he wouldn't have to work anymore, if he lived simply and within his means. His life sure wouldn't be extravagant, but at least it would be comfortable. He could just settle in and grow to be a blind old man with no worries. No worries? Now, that was a laugh. *Blind*. He didn't know if he'd be able to bear it. Sometimes, he wondered if he'd end up putting a slug in his skull in order to escape his impending world of darkness.

He sat up and opened his eyes, and the room came slowly back into focus. Well, the dresser did, anyhow, then the far wall, although both of them ran downhill when he looked with one eye closed. But he knew that when he went out the door, the hall would be in focus and even McMahon would be clear. Not like the old days, but clear enough. But the things going on across the street would be a fuzzy blur of colors and shapes and blind spots. If he walked out into the street, the end of the town, just three blocks away, would be a complete mystery to him. He had planned on this job being his last. Just getting on his horse and riding out alone was too dangerous for him these days.

Drug Cassidy had never been the foolhardy sort. He knew when it was time to quit, and this was just about it.

He turned the latch, stepped out into the hall, and went down the stairs.

McMahon, smiling amiably, was waiting for him in the lobby. He stepped forward and stuck out his hand. "Cassidy," he said.

Cassidy shook his hand reluctantly and said, "McMahon."

McMahon led them into the hotel's small but elegant dining room, where the waiter, bowing and scraping, rushed to seat them, and handed them two menus. Cassidy hadn't eaten here before. Something about dining in a restaurant owned by McMahon rubbed him the wrong way. But here he was. "So, what'd you want to talk to me about?" Cassidy asked, squinting at the menu.

Damn! It was bad enough that he was going blind, but the last couple of years he couldn't see close up, to read, to save his life. Presbyterian eyes—or something like that—his doctor called it. Said it meant "old eyes," a translation Cassidy found a little offensive. He held the menu out at arm's length.

"I've hired someone new," McMahon said, without preamble.

Cassidy didn't look at him. The stewed cabbage looked good. But then, so did the pounded steak. The roast chicken, too. Eyes on the menu, he said, "Yeah, you said you were gonna."

The waiter returned. McMahon handed over his unopened menu and said, "The usual, Paul."

"Yessir," came the reply. "Are you ready, sir?" he asked Cassidy.

Cassidy folded the menu. "I'll take the pounded steak dinner. With peas, if you got 'em, mashed potatoes and gravy, and plenty of coffee."

"Certainly, sir." Cassidy's menu slid away in the waiter's hands.

The dining room was painted and papered in dark green with mahogany trim, with dark green tablecloths and dark green napkins. Only the many ornate oil lamps and the crystal chandelier—which was just being hoisted back to the ceiling after being lit by two boys—and the large mirror at one end of the room kept the place from feeling like a unnaturally verdant tomb.

Most of the tables around his and McMahon's were

filled with diners, though, including one impossibly fat woman in a dull purple dress, who sat alone at a corner table. She kept looking at them, but every time Cassidy caught her eye, she quickly looked away.

"Shall we get to the meat of the matter?" McMahon asked abruptly, and Cassidy forgot about the fat woman in purple.

Cassidy replied, "I reckoned there was something more to this invitation than you wantin' to have company for a meal."

Idly, McMahon ran a finger over his water glass. "The point is that the man I sent for is here."

Cassidy felt his brows shoot up. "Already? Where is he? At your saloon?"

McMahon chuckled.

Cassidy didn't much like the sound of that laugh. There was no humor in it.

"Actually," McMahon went on, "I wired him in San Francisco. But you know that. You read the telegram, didn't you? I would have."

Cassidy nodded. There was no point in denying it.

"I thought so," McMahon continued, a hint of satisfaction momentarily creeping into his voice. "Turns out that he was quite close. On business. His assistant forwarded my telegram on to him."

Cassidy noticed the slight stress that McMahon put on *assistant*. He had the feeling he was being accused of something—for instance, being a two-bit operator—because he didn't have a goddamn secretary, but he kept his mouth shut.

"At any rate, he's promised to take care of our little problem on the morrow." And before Cassidy had a chance to react, McMahon continued, "Ah! Here's our meal. Thank you, Paul."

The waiter slid steaming plates in front of them: pounded steak with peas and mashed potatoes for Cassidy, and some kind of noodle and beef dish for McMahon. It smelled a little like sour cream. Which for some reason, reminded him of the fat woman.

Without thinking, he flicked his eyes toward her corner. She was gone, and the waiter was clearing her table.

McMahon picked up his fork.

Cassidy frowned. "This your roundabout way of tellin' me I'm fired?" Around a mouthful of noodles, McMahon mumbled, "More or less." He swallowed. "Of course, I'm willing to pay for your time. Would a hundred dollars be sufficient?" He salted his dinner, then forked in another mouthful of beef and noodles.

Cassidy, who had not yet moved either toward his food or his silverware, tersely said, "Not nearly."

McMahon stopped chewing. He frowned, and swallowed again. "What?"

"I said it ain't nearly enough," Cassidy said flatly. "I rode down here to do a job for you, and I'm ready, willing, and able to do it. It ain't my fault if you want to go callin' in some fancy San Francisco gun. Want to know the way I figure it? Since you fired me before I had a chance to do anything, you owe me."

For the first time, he saw something ugly cross McMahon's face, something without passion or remorse. He had known it was there, all right. But the sight of it—and the suddenness of its intensity and depth—startled him.

It passed in an instant, but it was long enough for Cassidy to realize that he'd underestimated McMahon. He'd figured that McMahon was just one of those Johnny-come-lately town-hungry types who wanted his name on everything, wanted to own everything. He wished he'd pressed Slocum about just plain plugging him.

After a long silence, McMahon said, "All right. I'll pay you."

"The whole five hundred," Cassidy said. It wasn't a question.

"Yes," came the answer. "Provided you stay in town. If I'm going to pay for a damned backup anyway, I want him around."

Cassidy nonchalantly shook out his napkin. "A backup? You mean, in case this new fella can't pull it off. Or ends up dead."

With no hesitation, McMahon said, "Precisely. And should that happen, Mr. Cassidy, and should you be called upon to handle the situation, I'll be happy to pay you if you succeed. And if you don't? Well, I won't have to pay you anything if you're dead." Smiling, he picked up his fork again and gently stabbed at his noodles.

Cassidy was far from his boiling point, if that was Mc-Mahon's intention. Besides, his pounded steak looked pretty good. He simply picked up his fork and his knife and began to cut his meat. "Nope," he said amiably. "Don't reckon you would."

17

By one o'clock in the morning, Cassidy figured it was safe to ride out of town. He had taken himself a two-hour nap, and while he didn't exactly feel all that refreshed, he figured that at least he wouldn't fall asleep in the saddle.

He made his way down the silent, empty street—no signs of life, except at the saloon—to the livery, and quietly tacked up his horse. Nobody was in the barn, just a few drowsing horses. The little closet where the hostler slept was closed up tight, and no light shown from beneath the door, although a few snores made it through the ragged wooden planks.

He led the horse out into the street, gave a last tug to the girth strap, then mounted up.

As he started down the road, he was a little concerned about making the trip at night. It wasn't all that far, maybe a half-hour or forty-five minutes out to the S Bar J, and there was a full moon. Or close to it. But still, his vision was pretty poor come nightfall—as if it wasn't bad enough in the daytime.

He figured he'd stick to the road like glue and hope for the best. He also hoped that Slocum wouldn't have some hot-shot, trigger-happy cowhand out there waiting to nail whoever came up that road toward the ranch.

He sure didn't want to end up shot full of lead, he thought as he left town, keeping a watch for prying eyes and shifting curtains. Not this close to retirement.

Once he had put a little distance between himself and the town limits, he urged his horse into a soft jog. Not fast enough to get him in trouble, but twice as fast as a walk.

The desert sure looked different when a person was traveling at night. It had been a long time since he'd seen it this way. The moon silvered the brush and prickly pear and barrel cactus and palo verde he passed, which threw soft pewter and purplish shadows over the rough desert floor, giving it a soft, almost pillowy look.

Every once in a while, small pairs of bright green eyes flashed at him, reflecting the moonlight. An owl screeched in the distance, and there were soft rustles of night-hunting things crawling around in the brush. He'd camped in territory like this, sure. But it had been a coon's age since he'd traveled through it at night. It was almost peaceful. Except for the fact that everything past a distance of forty feet or so was just a silver-gray blur.

As he traveled west along the road, he began to hear an odd jangle and creak up ahead. It sounded suspiciously like a rig of some sort. He reined in his horse and sat there, listening.

Yes, it was a buckboard, maybe a buggy. He could hear the single horse's hoofbeats and the creak of the wheels. The horse was walking.

He considered the possibilities.

If it was Crowfoot, well, they hadn't met, had they? He might have a chance to get rid of him before he even got close to Slocum. Slocum wouldn't like that, he supposed, since he was so damn set on getting to the bottom of this whole thing, but he couldn't find out anything if he was dead, now, could he?

Then again, it might not be Crowfoot. After all, what the hell would Crowfoot be doing in a wagon or a buggy? Four wheels wasn't the best thing for a getaway, especially when you planned to plug somebody like Slocum, who had those cowhands of Miss Becky's wrapped around his little finger.

'Course, it might be some rancher traveling home after spending a little too long at the saloon. An inebriated driver would account for the horse's slow pace.

He decided that must be it, and urged his horse forward.

He caught up to the rig—which proved to be a buggy, the kind that doctors or ladies drove—in less than five minutes. It crossed his mind that maybe it was the town doc, out on a house call.

Made sense.

Once he got close enough, he could see that the driver was a great big fellow, wide more than tall, and all wrapped up in a beaver coat to keep out the cold. He wore a slouch hat pulled firmly down over his head. The driver was concentrating so much on the road ahead that he didn't see Cassidy until he rode up next to the driver's seat.

"Evening," Cassidy said, and tipped his hat. And when the driver turned toward him in surprise, he added, in equal surprise, "Ma'am." It was the woman he'd seen in the café, the fat woman in the purple dress.

Well, I'll be double dogged, he thought, shocked. Triple dogged!

"I have no money," the woman said right out, and she wasn't smiling. She *whoaed* her horse, and Cassidy reined in, too. "If you are planning to rob me, you can just go on to the next person," she went on. "Also, I have a Colt pistol beneath this coat, and I am prepared to use it."

"I got no intention of robbin' you or harmin' your person," Cassidy said quickly, holding up his hands, palms out. "Just thought it was odd that somebody else was out here in the middle of nowhere, travelin' in the dark, hard center of the night."

"I'll have you know," she said, "that this is not the middle of nowhere. I know exactly where I am going, and it is imperative that I get there. You'll excuse me, sir?"

With that, she slapped her long reins over her horse's back, and said, "Get up, Mordecai," and started moving again.

Cassidy, not one to give up, kept pace with her.

"If'n you don't mind, ma'am," he said, "I'm wonderin' where you're headed," he said.

She didn't answer his question. Instead, she said, "I saw you dining with Mr. McMahon at the hotel this evening."

"Yes'm, that was me," he replied, and came to a quick decision. He added, "When a man offers to buy me a meal, I'll take it, even if that man's a certified skunk."

He'd made the right decision, because she laughed out loud, and dimples sank deep into her cheeks. He decided she was kind of pretty for a fat gal. 'Course, she'd be prettier out of that ugly slouch hat.

"I'm Drug Cassidy," he said. "Short for Drugman. Pleased to meet you."

"Yes," she said, and nodded. "I've seen your name on a paper at the office."

Cassidy frowned. "At the office?"

"Mr. McMahon's office. Did he by any chance fire you tonight?"

This gal had more on the ball than he'd given her credit for. He said, "Tried to. How'd you know that?"

"Because he always takes people out for a meal when he's firing them. I'm Evie Siddons, by the way. I work for Mr. McMahon."

This left Cassidy speechless, a fact which was not lost on Evie Siddons.

"I take it you're surprised," she said.

Cassidy nodded. "You could say that, ma'am."

"I work there because it's the only job I could find,"

she continued, "so don't go thinking that I'm some big fan of Tate McMahon. He's 'a skunk,' to quote you. He's a very self-absorbed skunk, too. He thinks he's so smart. He thinks I don't know anything, that all I do is the busy-work he hands me. In a way, I'm his beard, I suppose. But what he doesn't know is that while he's out, I have access to the whole office. And I use it."

She made a *tsk-tsk* sound and shook her head. "The idiot. You'd think he'd at least lock his private filing cabinets."

They came to the big palo verde that marked the crossroads.

Cassidy, impressed with her deviousness, said, "Miss Siddons, are you turning north?"

"Yes, I am, Mr. Cassidy."

"Good. Because so am I."

She cocked her head. "The S Bar J?"

"I know it's a little late to come callin'," Cassidy replied, "but I've got to talk to somebody out there."

"Mr. Slocum?"

Cassidy said, "Yup."

She reined her buggy around the corner. "Then, Mr. Cassidy, we shall go together."

Slocum rode Becky like there was no tomorrow.

He pounded into her as deeply as he could, and she gave out a satisfied little "oof" with every impact. Her long, sleek legs were pulled up and at his sides, her dimpled knees were at his shoulders, and her arms were outstretched like swan's wings, her hands gripping and knotting the bedding as if it were a life preserver.

Her lush breasts quivered like aspic with each of his thrusts, and the hard, swollen, pink nubs of her swollen nipples stiffly rode the creamy, soft, trembling mounds.

He felt the yearning and burning between his legs increase like a fire fanned by bellows, bellows he had no inclination to stop, and just as he burst into his own climax, he felt her arch beneath him, heard her make a sound somewhere between a groan and a strangled scream.

He thrust into her once, twice, three times more, and then collapsed upon her, still buried within her, his head pillowed on her heaving breasts.

He felt her fingers lazily entwining in his hair, felt her legs, slick with their sweat, slip down his sides.

She kissed his brow.

He lifted his head, smiling, and kissed her on the lips, slow and sweet.

"That was mighty fine, honey," he whispered at last.

"Mighty fine," she echoed softly.

"I'm sure glad ol' Pete moved back to the bunkhouse," he added.

She grinned lazily. "Me, too. But you know why I had to keep him up here last night, baby."

"Yeah," said Slocum, rolling off her at last.

He put his arm around her shoulders, and she cuddled closer and snuggled the bedclothes around her, throwing them over him, too. It was cold in the bedroom, even with all the heat they'd created.

He asked, "Want another blanket?"

"No," she said with a smile. "You're keeping me warm enough."

"Always glad to be of service to a lady," he said, and she gave him a playful swat.

"What?" he said, feigning indignation.

" 'Always'," she said, her lips pursed. "You said 'always.' You rogue. How many women have you said that to, I wonder?"

Slocum ignored her last question, which would have been impossible to answer without an abacus and a memory like an elephant's.

Instead, he nodded, straight-faced. "Ain't been called a rogue in a coon's age. Gotta admit I like it a lot better than some of the things I've been called. Makes me feel sort'a rakish."

She laughed. She had been laughing quite a bit lately. It was a good sound to hear.

He just hoped that after this Crowfoot hombre pulled into town from San Francisco, she'd still have a reason to laugh.

He hoped that he would, too.

Now, he'd never heard of Jeb Crowfoot.

He could see how McMahon had heard of Cassidy, who had quite a reputation. He supposed he could even figure how he'd heard of that flashy trash, LeGrande, who was now taking a dirt nap a couple of miles west of the ranch house.

But Crowfoot?

Was he somebody that McMahon had just stumbled over? Maybe he was one of those boys who talked big, but had never done much of anything.

McMahon struck him as the type to fall for that kind of line.

Hell, maybe he'd just heard of this Crowfoot from some traveling drummer. Maybe Crowfoot didn't even exist.

But McMahon had hired somebody who knew what he was doing when he had Jack Jamison killed, hadn't he?

The thought gave Slocum pause.

How he'd love to get his hands on the mysterious bastard with the cats marked on his casings. Didn't even bother to pick them up, the lousy prick. It was like he wanted to claim the kill or something, to say, "I was here."

But if McMahon had known enough to hire somebody that good, a real sniper, to shoot Jack Jamison from a great distance, then it was doubtful that he'd fall for some braggart, or listen to some gabby salesman going through town.

But still, it seemed right odd that McMahon had called

in LeGrande and Cassidy when he'd already used a proven man. Proven to him, anyhow.

"Someone's coming," Becky said, pulling him from his thoughts.

He heard it, too; the rattle of a rig pulling up toward the house. It stopped, then he heard the murmur of voices and a groan and creak of buggy springs complaining.

"Who the hell?" Slocum muttered as he leapt from the bed and yanked on his britches.

Strapping on his gunbelt, he signaled Becky to be quiet, then tiptoed from the room, toward the front of the house.

18

The five of them—Slocum, Becky, Cassidy, Evie Siddons, and the ever-present Tia Juanita—sat around the dining room table. Besides a big pot of coffee, Tia Juanita had brought out half a dried-apple pie, half of the pecan they'd pillaged earlier, and a platter of cookies. But Slocum, Becky, and Evie Siddons were the only three partaking.

Slocum was on his second piece of pie.

"Tomorrow?" Becky asked again, as if she hadn't believed Cassidy the first time.

He nodded. "That's what McMahon said. He said he was only keepin' me around for a back-up gun. The sonofabitch. Sorry, ladies."

"I might as well not have come," Evie said around a cookie. "It seems to me that you already know most everything, Mr. Cassidy. And considerably more of it than I do."

"Not quite, Miss Siddons," said Slocum, giving his fork a last lick. This time, he picked up a cookie. They were sugar cookies, and Tia Juanita made them precisely the way he liked them, real thin and crispy, and all golden around the edges.

"This Crowfoot, Miss Siddons," he went on. "Would he by any chance be the same man McMahon called in to shoot Jack Jamison?"

Evie Siddons sat there for a moment, staring at her napkin, before she looked up and softly said, "Yes, I believe that is the case."

Becky leaned forward, her fingers clamping the table's edge, her face suddenly dark. "You knew? You knew and you didn't do anything to stop him?"

Evie looked like she'd been slapped. She sat back in her chair, looked down at her hands, and after a short pause, said, "I assure you, Mrs. Jamison, I didn't know until well after the fact. And I couldn't go to the law. Our town sheriff is a joke. He's owned by Tate McMahon, anyway. As is just about everything and everyone else in town."

She looked up again, directly at Becky. "Tell me, what good would it have done to say anything? If I'd told you, Mrs. Jamison, it would have been the same as signing your death warrant." She sighed. "Mine as well. Mr. McMahon doesn't like anyone knowing his business."

"And he especially doesn't want anyone to know the real reason why he's grabbin' all this land up, does he, Miss Siddons?" Slocum asked softly.

Evie just stared at him, but Becky leaned forward, her eyes suddenly seeming twice as big as they had before.

"You know, don't you?" he asked Evie.

Again, silence.

Whether it was a bit of held-over, misplaced loyalty— or whether she simply didn't know—was a moot point. He answered for her.

"It's silver, ain't it?" he said. "Or gold. Or oil, maybe. There's nothing special about this land. No offense, Becky. But you could find just as good or better grazing land about anywhere. And he's makin' sure to snatch up all the mineral rights along with everything else."

Becky's brow furrowed. "And just how do you know that?"

"Oh, the other day I rode around and asked a few of your neighbors," Slocum said as he bit into a cookie. "Chatty bunch, once I told 'em I was stayin' with you. Also, a couple of 'em remembered me from the last time I was in town."

"You never told me," Becky said.

"You were off gettin' cheese or playin' in the flowers," he said with a grin.

"Oil?" Cassidy piped up. "There any money in that stuff?"

Slocum nodded. "Startin' to be. 'Course, it could be a fad. My bet's on bright metal. Evie?"

She sighed. "All right. Silver. He found a vein that starts east of town. He'd had three different geologists in—secretly, of course—and they believe that the vein widens by quite a bit, then branches off. It runs, they think, clear through town and as far west as the middle of your land, Mrs. Jamison. And as far south as the old McKelleps place, with several other branches in between, of course. So you see, Mrs. Jamison, he stands to become a very wealthy man, especially if he can control the whole thing."

"Call me Becky, Miss Siddons."

"Thank you, Becky. Call me Evie."

Cassidy, who had all but ignored the last exchange, stared at Slocum. "You knew all the time, didn't you, you big ox?"

Slocum shrugged. "Had a pretty fair idea. Branches north, too, doesn't it, Miss Siddons?"

The fat woman nodded. "Clear into the old Lightner spread, I believe." And then she sighed. "But what could I do about it? I was just one woman, alone, and McMahon was my only way of supporting myself. Indian Springs already has a schoolteacher, and Mr. Cleve at the newspaper only hires male typesetters and reporters. And please, everybody call me Evie."

"Evie?" said Slocum, and she smiled at the first name. "This Jeb Crowfoot that McMahon's got workin' for him now?"

Evie looked around the table, and her gaze stopped on Becky's face. Sorrowfully, she bowed her head and whispered, "I'm so sorry, Becky. Crowfoot's supposed to be a crack shot at a distance. I forget what they call them."

"Snipers," Becky said in disgust.

"Yes," said Evie quietly. "Snipers."

Slocum nodded, and Cassidy let out a sigh. Becky said nothing at all, but her mouth set into a hard line. Tia Juanita crossed herself, and her lips moved in a silent prayer.

Slocum turned to Cassidy. "And now you're telling me that he's here." He tipped his head. "Out there somewhere."

"He'd never sleep in a hotel," Evie said softly. "He's crazy. Thinks he'll catch some sort of disease, sleeping where other people have slept or touching what other people have touched. He wears gloves all the time, too. I didn't see him long, but it was long enough to find out that much."

She paused. "And he wanted his money in gold coins, in a pouch. The last time he was here, Mr. McMahon had to borrow the one from my purse mirror to put his money into. And Crowfoot chided him because he hadn't boiled it first."

"He's loco, all right," said Tia Juanita, as if there were absolutely no question that Evie was correct.

Not a single person at that table disagreed with her.

While Tia Juanita, Evie, and Becky were in the house, doing whatever three sleepy but keyed-up women did at three o'clock in the morning, Slocum and Cassidy shrugged into their coats and repaired to the front porch.

Slocum leaned against a porch post and rolled himself a quirlie while Cassidy sat down on the porch swing and lit a cigar he'd swiped from the humidor in the parlor. It was a good one. He didn't see many like it, these days.

Puffing, enjoying the flavor, Cassidy said, "So, what's the plan, ol' buddy? Kind'a like to know if I should put those horses up for the night or not." He tipped his cigar toward Evie's buggy and his saddle horse, tied farther down the rail.

"Put 'em up," Slocum said, cupping his hands around a sulphurtip, which he briefly held to the tip of his smoke. He shook out the match and took a long drag. "But later. Wanna talk to you first."

Cassidy slung both arms over the back of the swing. "Ask away," he said, the cigar clamped between his teeth.

"Your eyes ain't what they used to be, are they?"

Cassidy was taken aback by the question, but he didn't believe that he showed it, other than the cigar dipping a tad.

With a smile he didn't feel, he said, "What did you expect, Slocum? I'm gettin' old. Gonna be fifty-seven next spring. Hell, everything fades with time."

Slocum sighed. He pointed over his shoulder, toward the corral. "How many rails on that corral fence, Cassidy?"

"Three," Cassidy said right out. He couldn't see it, of course. He could only see a grayish blur. But he was pretty damned sure he remembered three rails.

"There's four," said Slocum, more kindly than Cassidy would have expected. "Your eyes are goin', ain't they, Drug?"

Cassidy didn't say anything.

He didn't know what to say.

"You seen a doc?" Slocum asked at last, breaking the silence. "Nothin' wrong with wearin' glasses, you know."

Cassidy brought his arms down from the swing's back and put his elbows on his knees. "Glasses ain't gonna help none," he said. "I'm goin' blind. Some kind'a deal I inherited from my ma or my pa. Don't know which one since they both died young, before they had a chance for it to happen to them. They was lucky."

Now it was Slocum's turn to be speechless. After a moment, he looked away, cleared his throat, and murmured, "I'm awful damn sorry, Drug. How long you got?"

Cassidy removed his cigar and studied the ember on the tip. "Four, maybe five years till I've gotta get me a cane and a pair of dark glasses, and have to ask people to help me across the street," he replied.

"But I can still be a help to you," he went on. "Just ain't got my distance vision no more. Night vision's kind of shot, too. But in the day, I can still hit a nickel at fifty feet."

Slocum arched a brow, and Cassidy added, "Well, thirty-five feet, give or take."

He propped his head in one of his hands. "Y'know, this was gonna be my last job. That five hundred McMahon offered me for pickin' you off would'a put my little nest egg over the top. I mean, I wouldn't have lived fancy or nothin', but I would'a been all right." He sighed. "Now it looks like I'm gonna have to take on another job, goddamn it."

Slocum stubbed out his smoke on the sole of his boot, then tossed the butt out into the yard. "Well, maybe we can just get that five hundred bucks for you after all, Drug."

Cassidy's features scrunched. "Just how the hell you figure we're gonna pull that off?" Slocum was a goddamn enigma, that's what he was.

"Tell you when I get it all thought out," Slocum said, and stood up straight. "Can you see well enough to help me get these horses put up and haul that buggy out back of the barn?"

Annoyed, Cassidy stood up, too, and jabbed his cigar back into the corner of his mouth, between his teeth. "Bet your boots," he said around it. "I ain't helpless yet, y'know. Nothin' like it. And I don't need no goddamn nursemaid."

Slocum grinned. "Fine. Do it all by yourself, then. Then you'd best get your butt back up to the house. We've got a lot of planning to do for tomorrow. And I don't know about you, but I'd like to catch me a couple hours of sleep."

19

After a couple hours of putting their heads together, and finally being satisfied with their plan, everyone, with the exception of Tia Juanita and Evie Siddons toddled off to bed. Tia Juanita had excused herself an hour into the proceedings, and yawned her way back to her quarters. Evie, too, had pleaded exhaustion, and was currently ensconced in the second guest bedroom.

Becky could hear the bedsprings creaking as Cassidy climbed into bed in the spare room previously occupied by Pete. Becky, herself, was alone in the master bedroom.

Slocum had ridden off somewhere.

He'd kissed her and said not to worry, he'd be all right.

She hadn't believed him, not for a second.

Fitfully, she tried to go to sleep, to make morning come that much sooner, but her eyes kept fluttering open, and she couldn't stop the wheels in her mind from turning, turning.

What had she gotten them into?

There was Slocum, of course, who was after all her hero, who was so kind and fair, and the best lover she had ever known; Mr. Cassidy, who seemed quite nice for a hired gun, and who she found herself liking very much;

and poor chubby Evie Siddons, who, despite working for that blistering rat McMahon, seemed a nice enough person. At least, she had come all the way out here in the middle of the night to warn them.

She stared out the window, snugged up in her quilt and feeling lower than a well-digger's boot heel, to quote one of Slocum's more colorful sayings.

What if it didn't work, this thing he had planned? What if he got killed, murdered just as surely as Jack had been murdered, just as surely as she suspected Cassidy and Evie would be when McMahon discovered their duplicity.

She should have talked Jack into leaving, somehow. Let McMahon have his blasted silver! Jack would have still been alive, at least. He was a kind man, a good man, and he was wonderful to her, even though she hadn't truly loved him. She'd liked and admired him, though. And that counted for quite a bit.

But then, how many couples had she met who were truly, deeply in love?

She could count them on the fingers of one hand, and still have fingers left over.

And after Jack had been killed, she should have pushed her stubborn streak and her pride aside and just sold to McMahon. He'd offered her a fair price. But no, she'd been too blasted proud to sell out to the man she was sure had murdered her husband.

Too proud! And now, because of that pride, all these people, these brave, wonderful people, were going to die, too.

She reached beside her, under the quilt, and once again touched the double-barreled shotgun Slocum had left her. She knew how to use it, and what she was supposed to do with it.

But that all depended on whether Slocum made it through the night.

"Oh, Slocum," she whispered as she began to quietly weep. "I'm so sorry."

Evie Siddons had not yet fallen asleep, either, and she was having second thoughts about sneaking out here in the middle of the night—about coming here at all—and about crossing Tate McMahon.

What if, in spite of Slocum and that nice Mr. Cassidy, McMahon won out after all?

Her goose would most surely be cooked, and that was all there was to it. At the very least, she'd be fired. At worst, she'd be killed, probably when she least expected it.

When she'd started working for McMahon, she'd actually liked him. Oh, she'd fallen for that tidy, bay rum, smiling facade of his, all right. It had taken her about two weeks to figure out what he was really like, which was about the time she had run across the first of those incriminating files, the files that proved he was as crooked as a corkscrew. And had just about as much conscience.

She knew that he was convinced she was in love with him. Men like Tate McMahon always thought that every woman they passed secretly yearned for them. But the truth was that she detested him and everything he stood for.

I am an idiot, she thought, frowning into the darkness. *A perfect idiot.*

Why hadn't she just pulled up stakes and moved to another town? The answer to that was easy.

Inertia. Simple inertia.

And there you had it. She'd been just too plain lazy to change her habits, to do anything different, to take a chance.

And now, at last, she had.

She had a feeling that she was going to pay for it.

• • • •

Drug Cassidy slept like a log, his face covered by his hat, his hand lying across his chest with his pistol, out of long habit, gripped firmly in it.

Tia Juanita had gone to her room, but she had not yet gone to her bed.

For the past hour, she had knelt before the little shrine in her room, all the candles lit and the incense burning for Our Lady of Guadalupe.

And she prayed for Slocum, for Miss Becky, for all of them.

Oh, how she prayed.

Slocum and Concho trotted slowly east. The horse nodded his head and fussed at his bit with unspent energy, and Slocum thought, not for the first time, that he should have taking Concho out for a good, hard gallop yesterday.

Oh well. Too late now.

He patted the horse's neck, whispering, "Easy, old son, easy," and reined him down a little slower. He didn't want the sound of his hoofbeats carrying.

Slocum had roused the hands before he left the S Bar J. Right now, several of them were sleepily fanning out in all directions, all traveling slowly and as quietly as possible, and all on the lookout for Crowfoot's campsite. He'd given them instructions, if and when they should spot him, to go directly back to the ranch and report to Cassidy.

He was traveling south, just off the side of the road, through soft sand that made less clatter than the packed and rutted roadway. And all the while, he kept his eyes peeled for any trace of a fire, or the tiniest wisp of smoke.

That would have been easy, wouldn't it? Crowfoot being dumb enough to build a fire, then not put it out all the way. But he had a feeling that Crowfoot was far from stupid. Crazy, maybe, but not dumb.

He had taken this route because he figured it was most

likely the way that Crowfoot had come from town. Of course, Crowfoot might have gone in a completely different direction, just to confuse the matter.

Slocum couldn't take any chances, though. He'd ride south, then turn east, near the road, and go most of the way toward town. Then he'd ride north about a mile, and cut across the desert, back toward the ranch.

He didn't really expect Crowfoot to camp right beside the goddamn road. He'd be off someplace. But Slocum was counting on seeing his horse's head above the cactus long before he saw Crowfoot.

He'd told the other men to go back and report, sure. But he wasn't sure what he'd do if he were the one to run across him first.

He wouldn't shoot him in his sleep, although he felt like it. No, he supposed he'd have to wake him up first, give him a fair chance.

He snorted softly. Fair chance, his ass. Like Crowfoot had given a fair chance to Jack Jamison.

By the time Slocum finally reached Indian Springs, it was nearing dawn. He hadn't realized how long it would take him at a walk or a soft jog. But at least the journey had taken some of the edge off Concho. He'd stopped shaking and nodding his head and pulling at the bit.

Slocum reined to the north, out into the desert, and started cutting up through cactus and brush. He had decided not to go a full mile. Maybe a half. There were low, jagged hills to the north, and he figured that once it came light, he'd be able to see all the way to their bases—and most of the way back to the road. The land there was fairly flat.

He hoped that Dave was having more luck than he was. He'd taken the southern route to town. Maybe Dave was already back at the ranch, shaking Cassidy awake.

Slocum grinned. He wondered if Cassidy still slept with that old Colt .45 gripped in his hand, under his pillow.

Dave had best knock first, and maybe he'd best give a holler on top of it. Cassidy had a tendency to shoot first and ask questions later.

It was a shame about Cassidy's eyes. A goddamned shame. Slocum couldn't imagine what that would be like, to slowly and inexorably lose his vision. Especially a man like Cassidy, who made his living bounty hunting and freelancing his gun.

Much as Slocum did.

A shiver ran through him, despite his heavy coat. He didn't want to think about it.

Having traveled roughly a half mile, weaving around prickly pear and cholla and the occasional palo verde or ironwood, he turned west again.

Morning was sending the first fingers of light over his shoulder. He kept Concho at a walk, and watched the desert.

Jeb Crowfoot awoke in pain, as he usually did. His left knee always started out stiff, from an injury he'd received falling from a galloping horse when he was seven or so. His right shoulder was still bum from a slug he'd taken in it. He'd tracked down the Mexican that shot him and made him suffer for an hour before he finally did him in.

His joints creaked and hurt, and he had a kink in his neck.

But he was used to it. A man could get used to anything, he thought, as he carefully and slowly got to his feet. He went through his morning ritual, making circles with his head and neck until the kink was gone, slowly rotating his shoulder while the pain worsened, then lessened.

Then he folded his blankets neatly—after shaking each one out for an inordinate amount of time—then rolled them all together and tied them behind his saddle. He watered and fed his horse, saddling it while it ate from the nosebag, and cleaned off every piece of saddle leather that had touched the ground with a soft cloth.

He used the same cloth to wipe his boots.

Next, he shaved carefully, and finished it off with a splash of witch hazel. The shaving kit put away, he pulled a pouch of hardtack from his saddlebags, throwing away a few broken pieces in disgust. No fire for him this morning, no coffee. Just hardtack and water. He had work to do.

After he ate two perfect pieces of hardtack and had a long drink of water, he removed the horse's nosebag and bridled it, folding the halter as neatly as he could, and placing it, too, inside his saddlebags. The rope, he coiled perfectly before he placed it over his saddlehorn.

Finished at last, he gave a thorough hand-dusting to his clothes, took off his gloves and shook them, put them back on, then mounted up.

He turned his horse to the west.

He was still undecided as to the best way to pull this off. Slocum didn't know him, he was fairly certain. Of course, he only knew of Slocum by reputation, but that was enough to unnerve him. A little.

He figured he had two options. He could simply ride into the ranch on some pretense or other, get Slocum alone, and kill him quietly, with a knife or a garrote. Neither was his style, really, and he hated the thought of getting that close to another person, let alone the blood if it came down to a knife.

The other option was to somehow lure Slocum out into the open, and shoot him from a distance. That had always been his stock in trade. He knew he was a very good sniper—possibly the best who had ever lived—although he was handy with a pistol, too.

He was handy with just about any implement that resulted in someone else's death, and he was proud of it. Perhaps too proud.

But how to lure Slocum out into the open?

20

Slocum was about fifteen minutes away from the road that went north, up toward the S Bar J, when he spied a flash of something from the corner of his eye.

Quickly, he turned his head and squinted, then yanked his rifle from its boot. In one smooth move, he leapt off Concho, smacked the horse in the hind quarters, then went facedown in the weeds.

The startled Concho took off running, but it wasn't quick enough. The horse hadn't gone fifteen yards before he screamed. And, as he stumbled to his knees, Slocum heard the report of a rifle.

Slocum gritted his teeth and swore silently as he scuttled and crawled toward the nearest shelter, a clump of prickly pear. It was useless for stopping bullets, but at least it was some cover. And as he flopped out behind the cactus, searching for a place to shoot from, he heard Concho groaning.

It nearly killed him to hear a horse in agony, especially when it was his horse, his Concho. But he could do nothing about it now. Concho was down in the brush about forty feet off. All he could see of the horse was part of

the stirrup leather, rising and falling as the horse labored
for breath.

And there were more important matters at hand. That
goddamn horse killer, for instance.

It had to be Crowfoot. It couldn't be anybody else. And
he had most likely aimed at the horse on purpose, to make
sure Slocum stayed put.

Damn his eyes!

Cursing, Slocum found a small space between two
prickly pear pads big enough to shoot—and see—
through. There was no sign of that bastard Crowfoot. No
sign, even, of his horse.

Slocum wondered if Crowfoot had trained the horse to
lie down. He'd heard of a few bounty hunters and shootists that trained their mounts to do that.

He knew that Crowfoot had to be there, though.

He was out there, just waiting.

Off to the side, Slocum's horse groaned again, a deep,
rattling sound, and Slocum was suddenly aware that poor
old Concho was going to die before he had a chance to
put him out of his misery.

Cold, hard rage coursed through his system, and for a
moment, he stopped thinking. He just aimed at a clump
of vegetation large enough to hide a man—or a horse—
and fired three times, quickly.

Nothing.

But the returned shots spattered into the cactus mere
inches from his head, and sent prickly thorns into his
cheek and forehead.

Ignoring the pain, Slocum fired twice at the next largest
clump, the one from which the shots had come: a grouped
trio of barrel cactus.

This time, cactus exploded and he heard a faint yelp.

No movement, though. At least, none that he could see.
And no shots were returned.

But Crowfoot was a tricky as well as a sneaky sono-fabitch.

Slocum didn't move. He aimed directly at the left-most barrel cactus, and fired three more shots, low to the ground, and going toward the right.

Shattered cactus sailed into the air. He saw a flash of fabric as it fell to the side, and a puff of dust as Crowfoot hit the ground.

Crowfoot was down, but Slocum couldn't be certain he was dead. He could very well be playing possum, waiting for Slocum to come check on him. It had happened to Pete, and it could happen to him.

But first things first. On his belly, he began to work his way over to Concho, who was still giving out strangled, rattling groans.

When at last he reached Concho, the gelding's beautiful leopard hide was covered in blood. He'd been shot through a lung, as far as Slocum could tell, and was help-lessly drowning in his own blood. There was no saving him.

Choking, Slocum drew his Colt. He stroked the horse's neck and scratched him on his forehead, where he liked it. And then he pressed the barrel of his gun into the hollow just above the horse's eye.

"Sorry, Concho, ol' son," he whispered. "You were one damn fine horse."

He pulled the trigger.

No sooner had he put the horse out of his misery than the horse's body jolted again. Slocum saw the entry wound, mere inches from where his gun hand had been, before he heard the report.

Shit!

He grabbed his canteen off the saddle, as well as an extra box of ammo from the saddlebag. Then, on his belly, he began to crawl back toward the cactus, careful to dis-turb the brush as little as humanly possible.

When he reached it, he stretched out on the ground, on his back, and reloaded his rifle. The magazine wasn't empty, but he was taking no chances. He wanted every possible advantage.

He figured he'd need it.

Jeb Crowfoot, bleeding copiously from his thigh, was busy tying off the wound with a fresh handkerchief. He swore softly under his breath. This was supposed to be an easy job. It was why he'd broken his rule about never going to the same place twice.

He should have listened to himself, because here he was, stuck full of cactus thorns, filthy dirty, and he was pretty certain that Slocum's lucky shot had nicked the artery in his leg. It was surely bleeding enough. It had ruined his britches. He'd have to throw them away.

That made him madder than the pain of the injury. That, and being dirty.

He hadn't seen anything since he'd fired that last, lone shot. Maybe he'd gotten lucky and taken Slocum out. The idiot had probably gone to shoot his horse, finish it off. Crowfoot knew he'd only shot it through the lungs. Enough to drop it, and enough to worry Slocum, if he was truly the horse-loving man he'd been cracked up to be.

Crowfoot had heard one story about Slocum strapping some fool across a big boulder, crucifix-style, and painting "Horse Killer" in the man's own blood.

He stuck a stick between his leg and the handkerchief and gave it a twist. It struck him that he'd best get on with things, or he'd bleed to death before he got his goddamn money.

He decided to take a chance. He'd seen no movement, so he had every reason to believe that Slocum was still over there, where the horse had gone down. He let go of the stick and brought his rifle to his shoulder.

He took careful aim, then fired a salvo of bullets at the site.

Slocum did a quick flip onto his belly when the shots started. They were coming from the brush to the right of what was left of the barrel cactus, but Crowfoot wasn't aiming at him. The shots were all headed toward Concho's corpse.

Without thinking, Slocum flattened out, steadied his rifle, and began squeezing off shots, aimed just behind Crowfoot's rising gun smoke.

He saw the brush shake with the impacts, saw twigs flying, saw whole branches sailing upward. He just kept firing, firing like he was a machine, not a man, and in no time half the brush was blown away.

And then he saw Crowfoot, or at least, part of him. Crowfoot wasn't firing anymore. Even from this distance, Slocum could see that Crowfoot's pants leg was covered in blood, and Slocum knew then that the wound had been from his earlier volley.

Slowly, he rose and began to walk toward the body. Or at least, he hoped it was a body, and not Crowfoot playing possum.

He doubted it, though. The closer he got, the better he could see just how much blood the killer had lost. If he was alive, it was doubtful that he was conscious.

At last he got close enough that he pulled out his handgun. He wouldn't need a rifle at this distance.

He walked up to the body slowly and carefully. Crowfoot was on his back, as jumbled as a discarded rag doll.

Slocum holstered his gun. Crowfoot had been shot not only in the leg, but in the shoulder, arm, and head as well.

He was good and dead.

Served him right. Goddamned horse killer.

Which reminded Slocum of Crowfoot's horse.

He whistled softly, and heard a nicker, but still couldn't

see anything. He walked toward the nicker and whistled again.

The horse answered with a whicker.

Slocum practically tripped over him, and what he saw made him sick. This horse hadn't been trained to lie down. He'd been tied, front and back, by short ropes quickly lashed around his pasterns. Then he'd been simply shoved to the ground, and his hobbled front and rear legs tied together.

"Sonofabitch," Slocum muttered angrily as he worked at the ropes. "You're lucky to be shed of that bastard, horse."

At last, he freed the last rope and the horse gained his feet, then had a good shake. Slocum picked the sticks and twigs from his hide the best he could, and only belatedly did he realize that the horse was an Appaloosa, having just five spots of white, each about the size of a baby's fist, scattered over his sorrel rump.

"Well, I'll be damned," Slocum said, and the horse nuzzled him in return, as if in gratitude.

He relieved Crowfoot's body of his rifle and sidearms, then mounted the new horse. He'd come back later with a spare horse—and maybe Dave, too—to get his tack and build a pyre over Concho. They could do whatever they liked with Crowfoot's lousy corpse.

He didn't give a good goddamn.

From atop his new Appaloosa, he spat down on the body. Then, absently picking cactus spines from his cheeks, he reined the horse around and started back toward the S Bar J.

Becky was on the porch when he rode up, and she ran out to meet him, crying, "Slocum! Slocum, are you hurt?"

He'd been thinking so hard about what was going to happen next, now that he'd killed McMahon's ace in the hole, that only then did he realize that he was spattered with blood. Probably Concho's.

He shook his head. "No. Got some stickers in me, though."

Cassidy, just riding in from the southwest, kicked his pony into a canter and rode up to Slocum. "What the hell happened to you, son? You must'a found all the trouble, 'cause I sure ain't seen anything but cows and coyotes. And a jackrabbit or three."

Slocum dismounted.

"And what in the name of Christmas happened to your horse?" was the next thing out of Cassidy's mouth.

"Crowfoot happened to him," Slocum explained, his face hard, his eyes cold. "He shot Concho, and then I shot him."

Cassidy's eyes narrowed. "The sonofabitch."

"My feelin's exactly," Slocum replied.

"Come up to the house," Becky said quietly. "Let me pull those thorns out."

"I'll see to your mount," Cassidy said, relieving him of the sorrel Appy's reins. "What you callin' him?"

Slocum shrugged. "For now? Just Horse, I reckon. Dave back yet?"

21

Later that day, while Dave, Cassidy, and Slocum were building a funeral pyre over the fallen Concho, McMahon was in his office, checking his watch for the thirtieth time.

It wasn't that he particularly missed Siddons, the fat cow. But there was no one to fix and fetch his coffee, or run down to the Chinese laundry to pick up his shirts, or pick up the mail, or to holler at, just for the hell of it.

This, he found quite annoying.

Also, he had expected Crowfoot to turn up, asking for his money by now.

Well, perhaps he was having a hard time catching Slocum in the open. There could be any number of reasons why he hadn't shown up yet.

Hell, McMahon thought with a derisive snort, maybe he'd had to stop and wash his damned gloves or something.

Crowfoot's money was waiting for him, though. One thousand dollars, all in gold double eagles, in two newly purchased velveteen pouches. He couldn't find one big enough.

He had nothing for Cassidy. He didn't expect to have to pay that do-nothing loser squat. Cassidy hadn't even checked in this morning, and his horse was gone from the stable. He'd probably skipped out during the night because he was too yellow to face McMahon yet again.

For some reason, this thought gave McMahon no end of satisfaction. He gave a haughty sniff and, to the clock on the wall, muttered, "Should have just hired Crowfoot in the first place. Looney sonofabitch. But he gets the damn job done."

He nearly shouted at Siddons to go pick up the mail, then realized once again that she wasn't there. Damn her, anyway! If she was sick, you'd think she would have sent somebody to tell him. That pimply neighbor boy of hers, for instance. Siddons lived in one of the little houses on Mesquite Avenue, about a half-block off Main Street.

Reluctantly, he scraped back his chair and got to his feet. He supposed he'd have to get the mail himself, goddamn it. He let himself out the front door, locked it behind him, and started up the street.

Their work finished, Slocum slid his orphaned saddle onto the back of the extra horse they'd brought along, for just that purpose. Behind him, Dave tended the blazing fire they'd made over Concho's corpse.

Crowfoot had really shot the hell out of him with that last volley. Slocum had had a hard time looking at him.

He snugged the spare horse's cinch and hung Concho's bridle, smeared with blood, over the saddle horn.

"You all right, buddy?" asked Cassidy, who had come up behind him.

Slocum had heard him coming. "Yeah," he answered without turning around.

"What you want to do about Crowfoot?"

Slocum had given it little thought, what with building Concho's pyre and all. He rested an arm on the horse's shoulder, and stared out toward the area where Crowfoot's body lay.

Buzzards had already landed, and he could see a couple of hungry coyotes carefully slinking in through the brush.

He said, "Nothing. Just leave him."

Cassidy moved so that Slocum could see him, and his brow was cocked. "You just wanna leave him for the scavengers?"

"Yup." Slocum's nose was full of the stink of burning horseflesh. He took the extra horse's lead rope and led him up to Horse. In one smooth move, he mounted up.

Slocum looked down at Cassidy from the considerable height of Horse's back. The Appaloosa stood sixteen hands if he stood an inch, and was one rangy sonofabitch. He handled smooth though, and so far, had proved to be fairly surefooted for such a big horse.

"Do me a favor," Slocum said. "Stay out here with Dave till that fire's about out. I know we dug a trench, but I ain't gonna be responsible for burnin' down half the Territory."

Before Cassidy could reply, Slocum reined his mount around and, leading the extra, headed toward the ranch at a jog.

"What if somebody comes?" shouted Cassidy.

"Nobody's gonna come," Slocum shouted back. To himself, he added, "Not yet."

McMahon came back from the post office, let himself into the office, and set his mail on his desk. Still no Siddons.

Damn her, anyway! He supposed he should have walked the fifty extra yards and gone to her house, but somehow, it didn't seem worth the effort.

Besides, considering one letter he'd received, he'd probably have fired her anyway, had she been there. He'd have no more need for a beard to cover the true face of his occupation. He could finally go into his real business—owner and operator of the new Silver King Mine.

That's what they'd call him, too, by God: the Arizona Silver King!

He opened the letter again and carefully smoothed it out on his blotter, reading it over twice just to savor the words.

The letter's sender was one George P. Lewis, a mining engineer from Colorado. He advised McMahon that according to his wishes, he had put together a crack crew of experienced miners, surveyors, and explosive specialists, and was ready to bring them down to Indian Springs, lock, stock, and barrel, as soon as McMahon gave the word.

Lewis also stated that they would be bringing a boxcar filled with equipment, and that he just needed a check from McMahon to get things rolling.

McMahon leaned back in his chair and laced his fingers behind his neck.

"Slocum dies today," he announced to no one. Satisfaction filled his voice. "And I'll wed Becky Jamison tomorrow. I wonder . . . should I send Mr. George P. Lewis a check and tell him to come ahead?"

McMahon smiled. "Oh, yes. I think so. Indubitably."

He had just finished writing out the check and was carefully blotting it when Sam Higgins, one of his so-called henchmen, came through the front door. He took off his dusty hat and cleared his throat. "Mr. McMahon, sir?"

McMahon began addressing the envelope. Without looking up, he said, "What is it, Higgins?"

"I don't exactly know, Mr. McMahon. See, Roy was riding out west of town when he seen smoke."

McMahon looked up, although with a touch of ennui. Frankly, he didn't care if the entire range burned. It was what was under it that he was after.

"Roy rode in a little closer and got out his spyglass," Higgins continued a bit more enthusiastically, now that he had McMahon's attention. "And he seen one'a the S Bar J fellas tendin' a big bonfire."

A bonfire? McMahon's brow furrowed. "Alone?"

Higgins shook his head. "No, sir. There was another fella with him. A stranger."

McMahon stiffened. "He wasn't riding a leopard Appaloosa, was he?"

But Higgins said, "Roy didn't say. Said he recognized the feller though. I mean, the stranger. Roy seen him eatin' breakfast over at the café the other mornin'."

"And you're sure he's not from around here?"

Higgins nodded. "Ol' Roy, he knows 'bout everybody and his dog what lives around town. That's why the feller at the café stuck out. I mean, that's why he noticed him in the first place."

McMahon held up a finger, asking for silence while he thought. Crowfoot wouldn't have been in town yesterday morning. He was riding in from Prescott or wherever it was he'd said. The only other two strangers in town would have been Cassidy and LeGrande. And LeGrande had flown the coop long before yesterday morning.

It had to be that scruffy little shit, Cassidy.

"Was this man nondescript?" McMahon asked, just to make sure.

"Huh?" came the puzzled reply.

McMahon gritted his teeth. "Was he ordinary looking? Not tall, not short, nothing special about him?"

Higgins shrugged. "Roy just said a feller. Didn't say nothin' more."

"Well, where is Roy?" McMahon demanded loudly.

Higgins jumped back a little. "At the saloon," he said. "He sent me. Said you ought to know. Said we was to tell you if anything different or, you know, funny went on."

McMahon stood up with a jolt, spilling ink over his freshly addressed envelope. He barely noticed.

He yanked his hat from its peg. "Come on," he said curtly, and opened the door.

"Where?" asked Higgins, rushing to catch up with Mc-Mahon, who was already outside.

"We're going to the saloon, you blithering idiot," Mc-Mahon said, striding swiftly down the boardwalk, forgetting to lock the office door in his haste. "To see that no-account moron Roy."

"Fire out?" Slocum asked absently. He was rolling something around in one of his hands.

Cassidy climbed up the porch steps. "Enough to leave it. Dave's still out there, though," he added, and sat down, perched on the porch rail. "Where are the women?"

"Inside," Slocum answered. "Why you think I'm out here? They're tradin' recipes or somethin'."

He managed a quick smile, the first one Cassidy had seen on his face since he rode out early that morning, before . . . before Concho.

Cassidy understood about horses. He was awful attached to his bay, Shorty, too. He even understood why Slocum had left Crowfoot's body for the vermin to dine on. He probably wouldn't have done it, but he knew why Slocum had.

"What you got there?" he asked, nodding toward Slocum's slowly moving fingers.

"Proof," Slocum said, and held out his hand, palm up. There were two cartridge casings lying in his palm.

"Same as killed Jamison," Cassidy said. It wasn't a question.

Slocum nodded, then looked over at the sun. " 'Bout four o'clock, you reckon?"

Cassidy checked his pocket watch, holding it at arm's length and squinting. "Five til," he said, and snapped the lid closed. "Why?"

"We need to get every hand positioned and ready," Slocum said, not looking at Cassidy, but out past him, toward the corral. "McMahon's got to figure he's about run out of options. You're gone, LeGrande's gone, and it ain't gonna be too long before one of his boys finds what's left of Crowfoot."

For Cassidy, light dawned. He'd thought it was revenge. "So that's why you didn't want us to bury him," he said.

Slocum nodded. "I don't know when he's gonna come, but it'll likely be tonight or tomorrow. He's gonna ride in here with every gunman he can beg, borrow, or steal. It won't be like that first day, when I broke up the wedding party. This time, he's gonna mean business."

Cassidy nodded.

Slocum continued, "Can you get every hand up to the house in about a half-hour, Drug? Even Pete. I know he's hurt, but it's his left arm that's stove up, and I can use his right."

Cassidy nodded. "Can do. Anything else?"

Slocum reached into a pocket and pulled out a middle-sized pouch. He tossed it to Cassidy, who caught it. It was heavy, and it jangled.

"What's this?" Cassidy asked.

"Eight hundred and change in gold. Took it off Crowfoot. Figured since McMahon wasn't gonna pay you, you ought to get somethin' for your trouble."

Shaking his head, Cassidy broke out in a self-effacing grin. "Thanks, ol' buddy." He gave the bag a little toss into the air, then caught it again with a swipe of his hand. It had a heavy, satisfying feel. More than satisfying. "My retirement money," he said, more to himself than Slocum.

" 'Fraid you've gotta finish earnin' it, though," Slocum added. "Sorry this deal turned out so rotten. For everybody."

"Seems to me you're the one who's lost the most," Cassidy replied.

"You're forgettin' all those folks who lost their land. And Jack Jamison, who lost his life. I reckon a horse, even a good-usin' horse like Concho was, don't compare to that. Not for most people, anyhow."

But as Slocum stood up and turned to go inside, Cassidy read something in his eyes. It was deep, deep sorrow.

And relentless, focused hatred.

22

It took McMahon two hours to round up all his boys, and by that time, it was nearly dark. He had called them in from the ranches and the bars, from the fields and the whorehouses, and he had given them the most rousing pep talk of all time.

They were smarter than Slocum, he'd said. They were tougher, meaner, more ruthless, and besides, all they really knew about Slocum was third- or fifth-hand, wasn't it? He set Slocum up as bag of air, nothing more.

And by the time they set out for the S Bar J at a swift canter, those men were pumped so full of horseshit and bravado that he could barely stand to be seen with them.

The idiots.

Well, perhaps, en masse, they could overcome this specter of a gunslinger.

McMahon had decided that surprise was the thing. Yessir, surprise that might well knock Slocum off that goddamn high horse of his. And Cassidy as well, that low-life side-switcher.

Nobody double-crossed Tate McMahon.

Nobody.

He didn't much care that Crowfoot was still out there,

looking for his chance at Slocum. Screw Crowfoot, anyway.

Of course, Crowfoot could come in handy, if they were to somehow entice Slocum out into the open. And if Crowfoot was within shooting range.

So he changed his mind once again about Crowfoot. He'd keep an eye peeled for him on the way out. He might yet prove useful.

After all, all they had to do was get rid of Slocum—and possibly Cassidy—and the battle was as good as won. And that last little piece of Indian Springs was his for the taking.

Not that he hadn't taken most of it already.

They galloped onward, McMahon's twelve whooping men thundering behind him.

Slocum was readying himself, too.

He had stationed men at various points around the ranch, although none more than a mile from the house. And he'd given them instructions to ride for home and not to shoot. He had looked directly at Pete while he said this.

Pete, his arm still in a sling, had the good sense to flush.

He'd kept back four boys, plus himself and Cassidy, at the house. And he'd sent the women, all three of them, back to the old Bar S and down into the cheese cellar. Becky wasn't happy about it, but she went, mostly because Tia Juanita and Evie Siddons threatened to sit on her if she didn't.

The men were stationed at various places around the yard: the big barn and the small barn, the edge of the corral and the bunkhouse porch. He'd put Cassidy out back of the house, and himself in the smokehouse doorway.

There was no one in the house, but he'd lit the cookfire and smoke poured thickly from the kitchen chimney. The lamps blazed, too, giving the house a warm, cheery look.

He leaned back against the frame of the smokehouse door, his nostrils filled with the scents of curing bacon and ham and turkeys and the ever-present dust, and rolled himself a quirlie, which he lit behind the shield of his hand. The sun had just set. There was no light in the yard save that which glowed from the front windows of the house.

He could see well enough, though. The moon was still close to full. And he could sure as hell hear well enough to know well in advance if a big troupe of riders came up that road.

He imagined that Cassidy, lurking in the shadows out back of the house, was thinking just about the same thing.

About halfway out to the S Bar J, a pair of coyotes sprang from the brush, causing McMahon's mount to rear and nearly throw him. He calmed the animal and stepped down to the ground as a third coyote skittered past, not ten feet from where he stood.

"Roy!" he called.

Hoofbeats plodded nearer, followed by a "Yeah, Boss?"

"This where you saw that bonfire?" McMahon asked. Maybe they'd been burning something dead. Maybe a steer. Perhaps the coyotes had been feeding on the remains.

"Nope," said Roy. He got down off his horse, too, and pointed toward the north. "Was off that-a-ways quite a bit."

McMahon scratched the back of his neck. And then he smiled. Maybe Crowfoot had come through for him after all!

They might have easily missed him on their way out from town. Now, wouldn't that be funny? Crowfoot coming for his cash while they were riding for Slocum's hide, and Slocum already dead!

He led his horse forward a few feet. "Roy, tell the boys to fan out. I want to see what those coyotes were up to."

"Check, Boss," Roy muttered, and McMahon, his gaze on the dirt road ahead, heard the creak of saddle leather as Roy mounted up.

It took less than five minutes to find the body. Or what was left of it.

McMahon was delighted! Well, Crowfoot had certainly saved him a whole heap of work, hadn't he? The man had earned every goddamn penny of that thousand dollars.

Of course, there wasn't much left of the corpse. Just as well, if you asked McMahon.

Until one of the boys said, "Hey, these gloves is still good! Reckon he won't mind if I take 'em, will he?"

McMahon froze while a couple of the hands laughed and the cowboy who'd spoken pulled off the corpse's gloves. One, he had to wrestle off the body. For the second one, he simply picked up the severed hand and tugged it free.

"Let me see those," McMahon snapped.

The hand, figuring he'd lost his new gloves, reluctantly handed them over. McMahon turned them over, looking at them closely. They were bloodstained and filthy and chewed up, but they were Crowfoot's.

Shit!

Suddenly, he tossed the gloves back to the hand, and the surprised man caught them against his chest, blinking.

"Back on your horses," was all McMahon said.

Slocum was still alive, dammnit. And he'd killed Crowfoot! Maybe there was something to all those rumors after all.

McMahon had never trusted too much in rumors. He came from back East, where such things, if invented in the first place, weren't allowed to get out of hand like they did in the West.

But perhaps, in this case . . .

No, he thought with a quick jerk of his head. Nobody could be that good. Someone had made an error, and that someone was obviously Crowfoot. And besides, he thought as he stuck a foot into his stirrup, what assurance did he have that Slocum had even done the shooting? Why, it might have been a random killing!

Or perhaps Crowfoot had stopped to clean his bleeding rifle and it had gone off in his face.

He couldn't even see a bullet wound. The scavengers had done a good job.

"Was it him, Boss?" asked one of his men. "Was it Slocum?"

"No," he answered curtly. "Just some stranger. Let's go, boys."

They picked up a lope once again, and went on their way, toward crossroads that would take them to the S Bar J.

Pete, favoring his arm, crawled up out of his sit and went to his horse. He mounted up and cut crosswise, over the range, toward where Dave was stationed.

Dave saw him riding in, and stood up, walking out from behind his cover of ocotillo and barrel cactus. "See 'em?" he shouted.

Pete rode up within speaking distance and hissed, "Don't holler, you lamebrain! And no, I didn't see 'em, but I sure heard 'em plain enough. Sounds like a whole passel of the bastards, too."

Dave led his horse out from behind its cover of cactus and brush, and swung into the saddle. "I'll go holler up Dieter and Toots and the rest."

"And I'll ride back to headquarters," Pete said.

"Check," said Dave, and reined his horse away, then stopped. "They comin' out the road?"

Pete nodded. "Just like Slocum figgered. Guess they didn't want to take no chances on the open range in the dark."

Dave nodded, then lashed his mount from a standstill to a hell-bent-for-leather gallop.

Pete sat there a minute, shaking his head. "Durn show off," he muttered, and reined his horse toward the ranch.

They rode into the yard as swiftly as a plague of locusts, and almost as noisily. As instructed, all the S Bar J men waited quietly, in hiding, for a cue from Slocum.

And Slocum? He just watched from inside the smoke-house door, waiting.

The boys from the range were back. Pete had ridden in ten minutes ago and given the alert. The others, who came later, moments before McMahon's men rode in, had taken up positions in the low hills that surrounded the ranch house.

Dave had signaled Slocum from the soft crest of land to the south, whistling a bird call, then standing briefly and waving his rifle.

Counting Pete and himself, Slocum had seven men down here and six up in the hills. He counted thirteen in McMahon's crew.

The odds were exactly even.

The mob faced the house. McMahon called out, "Slocum! Slocum, step outside!"

Now, Slocum figured that McMahon was a pretty easy target from here. He could knock him clean off that horse and directly to his maker with one simple shot. A ten-year-old kid with a decent eye could have done it.

But there was something in Slocum that had to give McMahon a chance, even if he was a bucketful of pond slime.

Besides, there were twelve other men sitting out there with McMahon, each one with at least a couple of guns and a rifle.

"Slocum!" McMahon called again, this time more boldly. "Come out here!"

Giving orders, now, was he? McMahon must think he had him pretty damned scared, all right. Except, hadn't he noticed that even Tia Juanita was quiet? Hell, on a normal day she would have stepped out on the porch and read McMahon the riot act!

McMahon dismounted, and along with him, four of his men. They started for the front porch.

Just before McMahon could put his foot on the first step, Slocum cracked open the smokehouse door.

"Stop right there, McMahon!" he shouted.

Every gun in that yard was suddenly pointed at the smokehouse. The click of hammers being cocked seemed like thunder.

Just as Slocum was thinking that yelling out had been the single biggest mistake of his life, McMahon smiled and held up a hand.

"Hold up, boys," Slocum heard him say in a voice filled with hubris. "This one's mine."

23

"You really think you can take me, McMahon?" Slocum said, a whole lot more calmly than he felt at the moment. He knew he could dodge to the left, to the shelter of the side of the barn, or right, toward the house. The barn was a long ways off, though.

Hell, he'd probably get shot with his first step, no matter where he headed.

"I do," McMahon sneered, his face lit by the lamplight coming through the windows. "You're not so damned tough. You're nothing but tall tales told by a bunch of drunken cowboys."

"I killed your boy, Crowfoot," Slocum drawled. He was still leaning in the doorway, but every muscle was tensed to leap to the side should anybody begin shooting. "Find him yet?"

Slocum saw the muscles in McMahon's jaw clench, saw his eyes narrow.

He added, "One of Becky's hands took out that fancy-dude shootist of yours, too. What was his name again? LeGrande, wasn't it?"

Several of McMahon's men looked at each other nervously.

McMahon's brow furrowed.

"Wouldn't be too quick to draw, Mr. McMahon," said a new voice: Drug Cassidy, who had come around the side of the house, effectively trapping McMahon between his gun and Slocum's. "Might be one'a them mistakes you don't live to regret," he added.

Slocum would have laughed if the situation hadn't been so serious. There were still a total of thirteen armed men in the ranch yard, all with their guns already drawn. They were scared now, but Slocum was well aware that sometimes frightened men could be more dangerous than brave ones.

"Now, don't go shootin' him, Drug," Slocum called. "Not yet, anyhow. Maybe we could have us a little parley."

"Parley?" snapped McMahon. Slocum could tell he was good and mad now. His face had taken on something akin to the color of a beet. "What the hell do you mean by 'parley'? I've got twelve men behind me. Looks like you've just got two."

"Three!" came a voice from the corner of the big barn.

"Four!" shouted another, behind the mob, from somewhere around the corral.

"Five!" called another.

"Six, you sonofabitch!" came yet another.

"I'm the seventh, and the one what shot your fancy man," called Pete from the darkness. "And there are about a dozen more, up in those hills. Just waitin' for an excuse to nail you."

By now, heads were turning every which way among McMahon's riders. Slocum could see a couple of the boys at the rear quietly backing their horses away from the mob.

Smart fellows. They knew it wasn't their time to die, particularly over a cause that wasn't their own.

But Tate McMahon was another case entirely. His jaw

working furiously, he did the last thing Slocum expected. Suddenly, he threw himself off the porch, at the same time firing his gun directly at Slocum.

Cassidy fired at almost the same instant, and took out the minion standing right behind where McMahon should have been.

Slocum fired, too. He thought he'd at least clipped McMahon, since he heard somebody shout in pain, but there was no time to think. He was running toward the side of the house, and McMahon's bunch were all firing.

Well, most of them, anyway. The ones in the center of the mob couldn't shoot without hitting one of their own men, and the two at the rear had taken off at a hard gallop down the road, joined a couple of seconds later by a third.

The boys in the hills opened up. Distant flashes of gunpowder rose into the night sky, and two of McMahon's men went off their horses and down under the milling hooves of their frightened mounts.

The rest of McMahon's men tried to get off their horses. Most succeeded. One was dragged, his foot caught in the stirrup, back in the direction of town.

All this happened in the split second it took Slocum to sprint the twenty feet from the smokehouse to the side of the house.

Once there, he dropped to his knees and peeked around the building, surveying the situation. All McMahon's men—the ones that were left, anyway—had taken cover behind trees or posts or the water trough or just lay plain flat on the ground.

For a long moment, the sound of gunfire was deafening, and Slocum shouted, "Hold it! Hold it! Stop shootin', dammit!" until he was finally heard and the shots petered out to nothing, the last ones coming from the hills like tardy firecrackers.

"McMahon!" he shouted.

No answer.

"Cassidy!"

"Ready, willin', and able," came the reply. "McMahon don't look to be in such good shape, though."

"You men who came in with McMahon!" Slocum shouted. "You can go. Nobody'll back-shoot you. Got my word on that. Pick up your dead and wounded, and get the hell out of town. For good. You got that?"

A murmur arose from the yard and the grounds around it, and at last, a single voice called out, "You really *are* Slocum, ain't you? For real and true, I mean. Not a made-up legend?"

Slocum groaned, but Cassidy answered for him. "He's the real thing, all right, boys. And you should get down on your knees tonight and thank the Lord Jesus that he was in a generous mood."

Slocum rolled his eyes, and he heard Pete—at least, he thought it was Pete—cough to cover a laugh.

"Get movin', boys," he said, easing around the corner. He leveled his pistol at the nearest member of McMahon's gang. "And before you get started, I reckon you oughta pile your guns out there in the center of the yard."

Bodies started to creep out from behind tress and bushes, from behind posts, and rise from the ground. Slocum heard the metallic *thunks* as men tossed their weapons in a pile.

The S Bar J men were coming out of hiding, too. Guns drawn, they formed a wide, loose circle around McMahon's men. Pete, his arm in a sling, had a great big smile on his face.

The rival gang began to sling the bodies of their dead over their horses. Two were wounded and just needed help mounting.

"You gonna take your boss, too?" Slocum asked.

"I ain't goin' back to town," one of the men said wearily. "Don't think nobody is. You can keep him, Mr. Slocum."

Just what I always wanted, Slocum thought. *My very own dead weasel.*

Except that just then, the dead weasel in question rolled over on his belly and fired, catching Slocum in the arm.

It stung like hell, but Slocum was mad enough that he didn't feel it right away. He simply fired back, purely on instinct.

His shot took McMahon right through the center of his worthless skull. He jerked just once, then went still.

"Holy Christ!" he heard one of McMahon's men mutter.

"And His daddy and mama, too," said another, pausing to cross himself. "Let's get the hell out of here."

In less than three seconds, the yard was clear of strangers, and all that was left was McMahon's body and a roil of dust.

The S Bar J men began to come forward, and the ones farther out began to ride down from the hills.

"Clipped you, did he?" asked Cassidy, just a little too gleefully.

"Shut up. I'm lucky you didn't clip me yourself, seein' as how you've got such great night vision and all," grumbled Slocum. He checked his sleeve. It looked like the slug had just grazed him, but he was sort of looking forward to the fuss the women would make.

"Shit," he said suddenly. "The women. Pete?"

"Yeah, sure," Pete replied. "I'll go get 'em out of that cellar, and I'll take Dave with me, if'n you don't mind." He grinned wide. "Bet them women smell like goat cheese by now."

Slocum smiled. He figured that Pete was right about that.

By the time Pete and Dave got back with the women—and Slocum had temporarily dragged McMahon's corpse to an empty stall in the barn—he and Drug Cassidy, who turned out to be a pretty fair cook, had drummed up a meal. It was late, and Slocum figured that if everybody else was as hungry as he was, there'd be a couple horses missing from the string come morning unless they got to work, and fast.

Tia Juanita stopped the second she bulled through the door and sniffed the air. "What it this?" she said suspiciously.

"Dinner," announced Cassidy. "Eat it or weep."

She sniffed the air again, smiling slightly. "I think I will eat," she said.

Next in was Becky, who ran directly to Slocum and kissed him all over his face and jaw, muttering. "Are you hurt? Did somebody patch you up? Was it bad? Pete said you killed McMahon!"

"Slow down, girl," Slocum said with a grin, noting from the corner of his eye that Cassidy had purposely turned his back. He had it bad. Slocum couldn't exactly blame him.

"I'm just dandy," he continued. "But ol' Drug there took a slug in the leg and didn't say a damn word. Got it fixed up fine, though."

Becky turned away from Slocum and toward Cassidy. He felt a pang of something akin to jealously, but quickly—and sternly—reminded himself that he was leaving. And first thing in the morning, if he knew what was best for him and everybody else concerned.

Besides, nothing against Becky, but he was getting a little itchy-footed. Time to move on. Time to find a new adventure.

Now he just had to tell her.

Evie Siddons had made her way directly to the kitchen without saying a word. She appeared at the door to the dining room bearing a big platter of fried chicken and wearing a bigger smile.

"My goodness!" she said. "I guess men can cook after

all! I wouldn't count on them having cleaned up the kitchen though, Tia Juanita."

Muttering in Spanish, the housekeeper stomped off toward the kitchen. Grinning, Evie placed the platter of chicken on the table, then went back for another load, probably the mashed potatoes or green beans that Drug had whipped up, or the pickled cukes and beets that Slocum had laboriously laid out on a tray.

Cassidy, making the most of his limp, allowed Becky to help him to the table.

And Slocum? Well, he just grabbed himself a drumstick. He was hungry enough to eat a buffalo on the hoof.

That night, in bed, Slocum made long, tender love to Becky. She came with a long, drawn-out gasp that spoke as much of sorrow as ecstasy. And when she had quieted, she began to cry.

Slocum wasn't exactly accustomed to this sort of reaction from females, and gently turned her head to face him.

"Honey?" he whispered. "What is it?"

"You're leaving, aren't you?"

He hadn't said a word to her yet, but somehow she knew. Women would always be a mystery to him.

At last he nodded. "Yeah. In the morning."

She pulled her head away and buried it in the pillow. "It's me, isn't it?" she said, through a muffler of linen and feathers.

"No, Becky, never," Slocum said, and he meant it. "It's me. I don't know why, but I've just got to keep movin'. Can't stay too long in any one place." He shrugged. "Just my nature, I reckon."

She looked up at him again, and her eyes were red and swollen with tears. "I know. I know, Slocum. It's just so . . . hard."

"Sorry, honey," he said, even though it sounded like a lame excuse.

But she said, "I understand. Some men are just that way. And you're the king of them, Slocum."

He ran his knuckles gently down her torso, following the rise and fall of her breast, the bell of her rib cage, the tininess of her waist, the flat of her little belly.

"And if I was in the market for a queen, Becky . . ."

She put a finger to his lips. "I know. But you'll never be. I guess I knew it when you rode in again. History repeats itself, you know."

Slocum grinned. "And we do have that."

She nodded. "History. Yes, we do. Slocum?"

"What?" He dropped his head to nuzzle at her breast.

"Just promise me one thing?"

"Anything, Becky. Within reason, naturally."

She sighed, her breast rising and falling dramatically beneath his lips. "Just promise that if you go—when you go—this time, that you'll never come back. Ever."

He raised his head and looked at her.

"I mean it," she said. "I don't think I could bear it a third time."

He could tell she was serious by the look in her eyes, and he said, "I promise, honey. You gotta promise me something, too."

"And that is?"

"That after I leave," he said, "you'll find yourself a good man and settle down, and be happy. Be awful happy. You're sittin' on a pile of silver, girl. You oughta be able to pick and choose. And you sure as hell oughta be able to do better than a beat-up saddle tramp like me."

She appeared to think this over. "Yes. I should, shouldn't I?" She grinned quite suddenly. "Pick and choose, I mean, Slocum. Don't look so wounded!"

He hadn't realized that his expression had gone that way, but he covered it quick with a wink. "Once more, honey?" he asked, and gave her nipple a little tweak.

"Already?" she asked, her brow cocked.

"Oh, yeah," he said, and slid into her again.

Several months later, while Slocum was spending some time up in Nebraska, waiting out the last of the winter with twin Mexican gals named Conchita and Maria, he got a letter. It had been postmarked and forwarded six ways from seven, but it had finally reached him.

It was from his old pal Drug Cassidy, and the original postmark was Indian Springs, Arizona Territory.

He didn't wait until he got back to the cabin to read it. He sat down right there in the post office, cozied up to the potbelly stove, and tore the envelope open.

He read it over twice, and then, smiling, he stuck it back in its envelope.

It seemed that the folks of Indian Springs had finally banded together into a real town. All the land that McMahon had bought or stolen was turned back to the rightful owners, due to a little creative bookkeeping on Evie Siddons's part.

The owners had then brought in a mining crew—the very one Cassidy said that McMahon had been in touch with.

The operation was moving right along, Cassidy said, and it was turning out fo be a rich strike. It wouldn't be too awful long before they started tunneling on the S Bar J.

But the news that had brought the biggest grin to Slocum's face was that Becky was now Mrs. Drugman Cassidy. They had wed about a month after Slocum's departure.

Now, part of Slocum was just a little bit pissed that Becky had taken him at his word, and that Cassidy had felt the need to move in so damned fast.

But those were small things. He'd never be back there again.

And now Drug would have somebody to take care of him when his eyes went, and Becky would have a good man to take care of her. And also, somebody who could cook pretty damned fine American-style food.

He stood up, stuck the letter in his pocket, and snugged his sheepskin coat around him in preparation for the outdoors. It was cold enough to freeze the balls off a brass monkey out there.

He picked up the bag of supplies he'd bought for himself and the twins, slung it over his shoulder, and went outside where Horse was waiting at the rail, his saddle dusted with drifting snow.

Slocum mounted, and set off toward the cabin at a slow jog.

Good for Becky, bless her heart, he thought. And good for ol' Drug. Good for everybody.

And especially, good for him. Conchita and Maria awaited, and tonight was bath night. For all three of them.

Grinning, he urged the horse into a canter.

Watch for

SLOCUM AND THE TEQUILA ROSE

298th novel in the exciting SLOCUM series
from Jove

Coming in December!